COSTLY HABITS

Costly Habits

Stories by Peter Makuck

University of Missouri Press
Columbia and London

Cataloging-in-Publication
data available from the
Library of Congress
ISBN 0-8262-1446-0

♾™ This paper meets the requirements of the
American National Standard for Permanence of Paper
for Printed Library Materials, Z39.48, 1984.

Designer: Jennifer Cropp
Typesetter: The Composing Room of Michigan, Inc.
Printer and binder: The Maple-Vail Book Manufacturing Group
Typefaces: Minion and Alcuin

Publication of this book has been assisted by the
William Peden Memorial Fund.

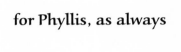
for Phyllis, as always

Contents

Bound Away   1

Under the *Azure Dee*   20

Filling the Igloo   36

The Price of Dining Out   54

True Colors   72

Existential Dirty Jokes   79

Simple Misalignment   96

Palliatives   106

Costly Habits   121

Bereavement Flight   143

Animal Planet   148

Yellow Tom   159

Junk Trade   172

Acknowledgments

I would like to thank the editors of the journals in which some of these stories or earlier versions of them originally appeared: *Crosscurrents:* "Simple Misalignment"; *Hudson Review:* "Costly Habits" and "Junk Trade"; *Kestrel:* "Palliatives"; *The News & Observer:* "Bereavement Flight"; *Ohio Review:* "The Price of Dining Out"; *Sandhills Review:* "True Colors"; *Southern Review:* "Existential Dirty Jokes" and "Filling the Igloo" (the latter was reprinted in *Selected Stories from the Southern Review,* edited by Lewis P. Simpson, Donald E. Stanford, James Olney, and Jo Gulledge, Louisiana State University Press, 1988); *Texas Review:* "Under the Azure Dee" ("How You Go Under"); *Yale Review:* "Yellow Tom" ("Persistence") and "Bound Away."

Thanks to George Core, Frederick Morgan, Paula Deitz, and Leslie Norris for their years of excellent editorial advice, encouragement, and friendship.

COSTLY HABITS

Bound Away

A car door slammed, then another. The noise startled, then angered him. Sitting up, Borden hung his feet over the side of the bed and stared at the wallpaper; faded roses came into focus.

In the dream, Chrissy was gone, but no note of farewell in purple ink lay on her pillow; he could hear her downstairs in the kitchen. Lifting the yellowish shade that initially made every day seem sunny, he looked down on the street, feeling mocked. The rain wasn't easy to see, but he knew it was there: maple leaves near the window quivered and jerked. Two figures in yellow rainslicks walked out of sight. Cars, as if at a funeral, lined up on one side of the street, all pointed toward the river, all but one—a customized van, gray-blue, aimed in the opposite direction. Borden glowered.

He was on the floor, counting and cranking himself up and down, when she came back to the room. Breathing hard, he stood up and slapped his belly.

She said, "Pushups won't take care of that."

"I know." He was thinking of the van. After a moment he said, "So, what's the weather report?"

"Radio says a hurricane is working its way up the coast."

———◆———

The days had been colorless, rainy, humid.

In the beginning, Borden had gotten up at the same time he always left for the job site, but instead had coffee at Krispy Kreme, checked the classifieds, touched base with the contractor he had worked for, then came home. Lately he had been oversleeping.

Walking into the bedroom, cup of coffee in one hand, cigarette in the other, he said, "How 'bout this friggin' rain!"

"Mmm." Chrissy was studying the makeup mirror, blue-lining her lids.

He looked at her neck, the jade studs in her ears. "Have you noticed anything funny on our street?"

"Funny?" Her eyes seemed to float on her face. "What do you mean funny?"

Borden knew she hated talking in the morning.

"Different."

She peered out the window. "I'll be late for work."

"See that van?"

"What about it?"

"It's parked in the wrong direction," said Borden.

"So?"

"And it's been in that same spot for close to a week."

Chrissy looked at his feet. "What are you wearing those clodhoppers in the house for?"

Borden looked down at the steel-toed work shoes with thong laces, dusty and yellowish. "Luck," he said.

She put her hand out for the cup. "Let's have a sip."

He handed it to her. "Keep it."

"The cars are student cars. The university's right around the corner."

He widened his eyes. "No—kidding!"

———◆———

The street was in an old neighborhood and arched over by huge maples and oaks. The Chevy van had a Plexiglas sun roof and a teardrop window at the back; an orange sunset and three green palms were pop-styled on the side panel. Nickeled Turbo Master wheels, spoiler, roof rack, laker pipes. Fastened to the back door, a chrome ladder climbed to the roof.

Parking was permitted on one side of the street only, and Borden liked all the cars pointed in the same direction.

I could just pick up the telephone, he thought.

Returning from Krispy Kreme with the morning paper, he noticed the Jersey plates. The van, from his home state, was down here in the coastal south, parked in the wrong direction, giving Yankees a bad name. And having to make house payments didn't improve Borden's mood, especially when, as now, he entered by the back door and decided to check the basement—flooded again. Great! Only two weeks ago he had pumped it out, dried it with a squeegee, but there was so much water in the sea-level soil that the floor, the very next day, was again a reflecting pool.

Standing water made the upstairs more humid; mildew skulked in the dining room and closets. In the bedroom a dehumidifier clicked on and off, keeping him awake.

The sump pump had to be fixed, foundation trenched, exposed, and waterproofed with sealer and sheets of polyethylene. Somehow Borden couldn't face the task; even the thought made him weary.

He put on his yellow rubber boots and waded toward the portable electric pump he kept in the crawl space. Walls were raining bile-colored flakes. A previous owner thought the answer to leakage was simply to paint the inside wall. One of those rip-off commercials ran regularly on TV: "Water in your basement?" Then the guy with a pencil mustache and a gaudy sports jacket held up a gallon can and punctuated his spiel with gestures that were forced and out of sync. *Just dial this toll-free number. . . . All major credit cards . . .*

Shit. But at least the guy had a job.

Borden opened a head-high window. Pulling in the plastic garden hose, he attached it to the small blue pump and moved the pump to a point where the water was deepest. He looked at the outlet, then decided it might not be a good idea to be standing in water when he plugged into the socket.

On the basement stairs, he thought of his mother, already three years dead. She used to say, *A house is a slow thief.*

Instead of rain, it was threatening rain. Gray. The hurricane was far down the coast, for the moment stationary. A motorcycle was parked in front of the van, a red Yamaha. Actually the bike had been there yesterday, but Borden didn't make the connection until he saw the guy step out of the van, yawn, scratch himself, and pull on a camouflage poncho. "Chrissy."

"What?" she said, faint irritation in her voice.

"Look at this."

"Whoopee! A guy on a motorcycle!"

"Not any guy," said Borden. "It's the guy who owns the van."

"Really?"

"I just saw him get out."

Chrissy said nothing.

Borden said, "I think he's living there."

Chrissy said, "He probably is. Paper last night said college dorms were full. Housing's short this year."

"It said that?"

"No, I made it up," she sang from the stairs.

Borden followed her. "Hey, like I care where they sleep, but the friggin' university ought to provide parking."

"Students can't afford a permit."

"Can't afford? Oh, my bleeding heart!"

The front door slammed.

Borden pounded his fist on the top of the kitchen counter, then stared at a black phone stuck to the wall.

Hands in his pockets, whistling, he idled toward the van, letting his eyes travel along branches of a huge oak toward an imaginary squirrel. This other side of the van had a picture window with red curtains cinched in the center, each shaped like an hourglass. A table, small sink, and a sofa of wine-colored bordello velour. A lamp with a red tassel shade. Lots of shag carpet. Gritting his teeth, Borden walked toward the river. "Can't afford a parking permit? Are you shitting me?"

The street's tunnel of trees ended at the water; a cement promenade with a black iron railing followed the shore toward big old mansions at the point. The air was heavy with a scent of brine. A row of imported palms dangled their brownish fronds, seemed ready to give up. Across the choppy sound was a barrier island. Once, near dark, he saw a great silver fish, what he thought was a tarpon, clear the water four or five times in a row. Another time he had seen a deer swimming toward the island. Today he wanted to see something, but knew he wouldn't.

He headed back to the house. If this area took the brunt of the storm, it would be Matchwood City; on the other hand, he'd be back to work immediately, and for a long time.

The woman on the Weather Channel pointed to a swirling cloud with a ragged white eye superimposed on a coastal section of the state map. The white swirl moved slightly left and right with each new satellite photo, but it wasn't going anywhere. "Like most women," she said, "Hurricane Diana can't make up her mind."

Borden went to the front window. The street pulsed with blue light from a black-and-white cruiser. A policeman was slipping a ticket beneath the van's wiper.

Borden plucked another cigarette from his pack and smiled. "Ahh, what a shame!"

They made love that night. Afterward Chrissy read, a little plastic lamp clipped to her novel. Borden went downstairs to check the late weather report: the hurricane was again moving toward him. He had a beer, flipped channels, and then went up to bed. The air was humid, his skin sticky. A sharp metallic pop came from across the street; Borden decided an acorn had fallen from the oak tree and hit the van. On his belly, he parted the curtains and peered between bars of the headboard. A light was on in the van, but its curtains were drawn. Muffled voices. "You know," said Borden, "Van the Man is not alone down there."

Giggling and soft music floated up.

Chrissy rolled to her stomach. "What are they doing?" she asked.

"Guess?"

"That's probably just the radio," she said, rolling onto her back, but throwing one leg over his butt.

Thunder rolled, lightning slumbered in the treetops, briefly sketching fast-moving clouds. Then rain pelted down, and it was all he could hear. Three small orange lights spaced along the van's laker pipes went out, but the teardrop window kept its soft melon tint.

A preacher stared at him and shouted. Spit flew. Helpless, Borden sat with F. M., the builder he had worked for. F. M. whispered, "This man is inspired. He knows the why of weather."

The preacher said it was a judgment; he punched the book.

F. M. said, "Amen," and nudged Borden.

Borden said, "Forget it."

The preacher said, "Thursday, Friday, Saturday—Monday, Tuesday, Wednesday."

F. M. yelled, "You left out Sunday."

The preacher shouted, "No, brother, you left out Sunday." Then he read: " . . . the wind goeth towards the south, and turneth about unto the north; it whirleth about continually, and the wind returneth again according to his circuits. All the rivers run into the sea; yet the sea is not full . . ."

Borden told F. M. that Death was a Baptist preacher and then, in the depths of sleep, slowly realized he was dreaming.

When he woke, Chrissy was gone.

He parted the curtains. The neighborhood was oddly sunny. The van was still there. He hurried downstairs and turned on the TV. The weather woman was pointing to the hurricane, still more than a hundred miles away, farther out to sea, but moving in a northerly direction. The sunlight—Borden could see from the satellite photo—was simply a small "window" in thick cloud cover. In fact, when he returned from the kitchen with his coffee and cigarette, the sun had disappeared.

Deep in an armchair, he puffed on his cigarette and watched his smoke rope toward the ceiling.

The showroom in Dodd's Lumber had plate glass double X-ed with duct tape. It was crowded. People buying $7 \times 4'$ sheets of $1/4''$ plywood for boarding windows. Borden stood waiting his turn at the register. Between buildings across the street a segment of the bridge was visible. Two old-timers were talking about the island and the storm. One said bids were out on a complex of condos at West Island Harbor, big job. The other snorted, looked through the window, and said it would be good if that bridge were gone, the ferry put back into service. Things had gone too fast.

Condos and honky-tonk. A motorcycle gang murdered some-body out there last summer. Eyes wrinkled like one of the island's loggerhead turtles, the old guy glanced at Borden and said, "What that ahland needs is a good harrykin."

The other laughed, "Re-zone an' start afresh."

"A-men!"

Borden bought two big sheets of plywood to have ready for the front windows—just in case—and two Skilsaw blades. Outside, he unlocked the Truk-Mate box fastened to the bed of his battered Datsun pickup and set the blades inside. The sheets he hooked to post slots with bungee cords, then turned and faced the sound. Water between houses showed white chips, flying foam.

The red Yamaha was gone. Rain slanted in sheets when she stepped out of the van and hustled down the street toward the university carrying one of those green tote bags. For a few mo-ments after, he fell to staring at a tropical orange sunset on the back side of the van. The sun was a taunt. The van receded but left behind a picture of palms and setting sun to float above the street, the sun stretched and slightly diffused, like a tropical fish. The tropics. He had always wanted to live far south, the Florida Keys, but would settle for a secluded place on the sound side of the bar-rier island. Real estate was cheaper on the sound side. Buy two lots, one of them a hedge for privacy. Build when he had saved enough money.

The van was gone—a beautiful empty space between a red Pin-to and a Rabbit. Borden raced from room to room. He'd park his Datsun in the spot and force the van to move farther down the street. Upstairs, in the bedroom, just as his fingertips touched the pickup keys on his night table, he could see the van moving slow-ly down the street. Now it was backing into the old slot, as if the space were reserved. He swore and went closer to the window. Then he left and returned with binoculars that just about brought her into the bedroom, freckles and all. Pretty and looking like a film star whose name he couldn't recall, she was eating a Wendy's burger (the yellow drink cup with red logo, hoisted periodically, told Borden that). Opening the door, leaning down, she put the cup on the pavement. For a while, she bobbed her head to music, waiting for the downpour to stop. Then she marched off, the bright yellow cup unforgivably left on the blacktop; the cup dominated everything in sight.

He ran downstairs and out the front door, yelled, but she had already turned the corner.

"God damn it," he said, sloshing the rest of the Coke on the van. After looking about, he impaled the cup on the van's antenna, and at that moment the sky opened, soaking him before he could cover half the distance to the front porch. Under the drumming roof, he stood and faced the van, astonished. Rain pellets hissed, covering the tar like white smoke.

Sissy Spacek—that's who she looked like.

Borden apologized, Chrissy listened. He had intended to cook something but got hung up.

Chrissy wiped her mouth and put down her hamburger. They were in Wendy's. "Hung up? What do you mean hung up?" she asked.

Borden explained about the paper cup Van's girl threw into the street. He explained that Mrs. Constable, the widow at Number 46, had seen something on her morning walk, and that was why he had to call their lawyer neighbor at the end of the street.

Chrissy shook her head. "What did Mrs. Constable see?"

"She saw Van the Man, zipping himself up."

"Zipping himself up."

Borden didn't like the echo. "Wait a minute. First of all, Mrs. Constable stopped *me* this afternoon. She asked *me* if I noticed the van. Other people have eyes too, you know?"

"Did she come to our front door?"

"No, I met her down on the promenade."

"So?"

"So, she thinks it's unsanitary. She thinks Van is using the street as a toilet. And listen, I didn't even tell her about Van's girlfriend."

"But how does our neighbor, lawyer What's-his-face—"

"—Knox."

"—Knox get into this?"

"He's the only one in our neighborhood with any clout. He says he's been wanting to get an ordinance against street parking anyway, because our street's too narrow."

Chrissy's face loosened, became tender. A tendril of her pinned-up hair had fallen and stuck out from her ear. And her white blouse, from work and humidity, had a wilted look.

"I'm sorry. You're tired." He touched her hair back into place. "But what do you think?"

She sighed, smiled. "I think you're a real case."

Chrissy made popcorn and they watched a movie. National Weather Service banners at the bottom of the screen kept them posted on the location of the hurricane. Borden had a few beers but was still restless. He went into the front room to peek at the van. No lights were on inside, and the red Yamaha was gone. The local news had shown several hurricane parties in downtown bars, students, glassy-eyed, grinning and hoisting beers, while merchants were taping plate glass, and people in oceanfront homes were boarding up windows. "What's it doing?" asked Borden, coming back into the TV room.

"They don't know," said Chrissy. "It goes a little this way, a little that way. Nobody wants to make any guesses and be wrong."

"Meanwhile, rain."

"Let's have a sip."

Borden handed her the can.

"Sit down." She patted the sofa and winked. "Give Mama a great big sloppy kiss." It was a line from the movie they were watching.

Thud.

He sat upright in bed. Chrissy lay on her side.

Thud. Down in the dark street, another door slammed. Voices—they leaped at the window, fell, leaped again. He heard the sliding door of the van, giggles. "Hey!"

"Hey!"

"You scared of a little biddy wind storm?"

Then Borden couldn't make out any more. He lay down again and edged toward sleep, but a burst of loud laughter pulled him back. The voices leaped again, like the dog at the back fence before he called Animal Control. Now this, the clank of a thrown can.

He'd have to kick ass—no two ways about it. He eased out of bed and quietly crossed the room. Hopping on one foot, falling into the dresser, he slid on his jeans. He waited, but Chrissy did not wake. More laughter came from beyond the bedroom window.

"Oo-kaaay!"

Borden laced his steel-toes.

Across the landing, down the stairs, through the front room, he reached the porch just in time to watch the car and the van turn right at the end of the street.

Rain had played its sleepy tune all night on the roof, but Borden shunned the basement, his ritual with the pump. This morning he had something more pressing. By now he knew Van's departure time and had the pickup turned around and aimed toward the street. With the window down he could hear the Yamaha snarl to life.

He followed at a distance. The river burst into dark oily segments whenever a field or wall of trees fell away. They passed tall grain elevators and corrugated silage bins. Once beyond city limits, even before Van cleared the gate and the security guard at Unitron Systems, Borden was almost sure, sure the guy wasn't a student.

On the way back, to celebrate the rightness of his hunch, he stopped for eggs and sausage at Elmo's, a twenty-four-hour gas station/rib shack where the owner, a wrinkled black man with white hair, wore a holstered nickel-plated revolver and made a living selling tires, moonshine, and fried chicken over the same counter. Borden watched the pistol shake as the guy scrambled eggs and wondered if private investigating was anything like this. He was still young enough for a different career.

After dinner, while light was left and no rain was falling, Borden went for a walk. Students were parking cars and hurrying toward night classes. The promenade was almost deserted. He stopped to see what an old guy had in his cooler. "Blues," said the man. "Dey be comin' in now, but dat 'ere harrykin no good foam." Two years down here, sometimes Borden still couldn't catch the words. Out on the island, lights were coming on, amber pinpricks. "Harrykin nuddin' ta mess wid." While the old man talked about storms he had seen, Borden watched a trio farther down the walk. Two guys and a girl. The guys were seated on the wall, probably drinking beer. Borden finally broke the old man's monologue. "Catch a big one for me," he said and idled on. He kept watching the trio.

As he drifted toward them, the girl broke off kissing the guy with the cowboy hat and danced to the black pipe railing. He whistled as she did a ballet move. Then she turned and lifted her sweatshirt, flashing her bare breasts. She seemed to be dancing to inaudible music. The guys taunted her. Borden slowed. She leaned against the railing. Looking over her shoulder toward the wall, she unbuttoned her jeans and slid them down, first showing only a coin-slot of cleavage, then left, right, until the jeans were at her thighs, and nothing was between her sweet tail and Borden's eyes but hot, heavy air. "You can kiss this," she chanted.

"Bring it over," said the second guy, "I'll kiss it."

When Borden thought about it later, he should have known better than to expect much of Knox. Not an ass-kicker like so many lawyers up north. Knox was thin and fond of cardigans, had wire glasses, and puffed on pipes; he was a reticent, gentle, family man. Friendly, he introduced himself to Van The Man as Jimmy, Jimmy Knox.

It was early evening. Knox held a folded blue umbrella. Van was seated on the shag carpet in the open doorway, picking a guitar, his fingers skillfully getting around the frets, making faint ghostly squeaks as he clutched and dragged between chords. He had blond hair, a face that was fond of itself, and good shoulders. The girl had sandy hair and sat behind him in the swivel bucket seat; she wore safari shorts and a slogan T-shirt that showed a winged foot and said, "Foot Power." Both were well tanned: beach-born deities. Van casually introduced Susie. Everyone shook hands.

Van had to have known the neighborhood delegation was coming. His story, well polished, was that he and Susie were getting married right after graduation in December. Van needed only six credit hours; he was taking courses at night and worked during the day as a janitor at Unitron Systems out on the bypass. Susie

was still full time at the university. The information came care-
lessly, as Van strummed and picked intricate little runs. They were
next in line for an apartment at River Bluff Estates, but would move
that night if their parking in the street were a problem. They chose
this street because it was in a good neighborhood and felt safe. But
even here, you couldn't be sure. Somebody a few days ago had
jammed a soda cup on the van's aerial and twisted it out of shape.

Borden looked down at his work shoes.

Van said, "Y'all ought to come hear us at The Club." At some
point in the encounter, New Jersey had imperceptibly disappeared from his voice.

Knox said, "When you playing?"

Van said, "Tomorrow night at eight."

Knox asked for a sample.

Van noodled, found a melody, and Susie came in just at the
right point: "Shenandoah, I long to see you . . ." They were good.
When the song arrived at "Farewell, my love, I'm bound to leave
you," Borden noticed Jimmy's eyes were misty and threatened to
brim.

Walking away, Jimmy said, "Nice kids. Right pretty song, wuddn't
it?"

Borden said it was.

The eaves whispered with soft, steady rain.

Borden and Chrissy made love. It was late, and she fell quickly
asleep. Borden stared for a long time at the ceiling. Making love
to Chrissy seemed to put her further from his reach. A dream he
had been having put her ahead of him on the promenade; the
faster he walked, the further she receded. But tonight, sleep was
elusive. He went downstairs and turned on the TV: damage re-
ports began to arrive from South Carolina. Beer in hand, he
watched footage of a beach house drifting out to sea, transform-

ers showering sparks, wind-crazed palm trees, flooded streets, people on the roofs of houses awaiting rescue.

Van—that fake southern accent, the song, the slick story—ole Van was smooth as a suppository. That dentless, glossy van. Borden felt mocked, beaten. Wind gusted and rain drilled the windows. He got another beer and changed channels: NFL players were holding out for megabuck contracts. Player reps and owners were making progress. Borden groaned. He switched to the movie channel, lay down, and pulled a cheap Mexican blanket over himself. On the screen, a gray-haired, refined-looking actor with a blazer, paisley ascot, and British accent was selling a two-record set of The World's Loveliest Melodies. He listed composers to a background medley of familiar classical phrases. "Mozart, Chopin, Rachmaninoff, Beethoven . . ." It was like counting sheep. "Strauss, Ravel, Berlioz . . ."

His back ached from the lumpy sofa. Chrissy had gone to work without waking him or leaving a note. It was dark and rainy. He had a coffee at Krispie Kreme, then took the bridge out to the island. Boats on the inland waterway leaped wildly at their tethers. The sky was the color of eggplant. In the boat launch parking lot was a red van; a young couple with a child was watching the storm-show. Two brown pelicans hunched on a black remnant of wrecked pier; they brooded and seemed to be watching a black ash-can buoy clock back and forth, faster and faster, in the terrible undertow.

Just the sight of her nightgown lying on the unmade bed made Borden quicken with desire. He hung it in the closet and made the bed.

Rain, rain, the whole morning.

The van glistened, an ice-blue ache.

He tried to imagine Chrissy at the bank. Computers—he barely knew what she did.

The doorbell rang.

Two young men stood at the bottom step: dark trousers and white shirts, black ties. "Hi, there."

Borden sighed.

"How are you today, sir?"

Each had a fat accordion briefcase.

"Come on," said Borden, "what's the pitch?"

Both flashed idiotic smiles. One said, looking at the dark sky, "We live in terrible times." The other ventured, "Have you ever wondered why Jesus put you here?"

A few minutes later, head aching, two aspirins swallowed, stretched out on the sofa, Borden wished he had said, "Yes, to insult morons like you." Of course he hadn't, and it irked him that a good zinger always arrived too late.

The doorbell again.

In a sleepy fog, he saw himself rise from the sofa, sure the God-sellers were back, but Susie, the girl from the van, made him catch a breath. Borden showed her into the kitchen, pointed to the phone, rubbed his eyes, and withdrew. Feeling terribly heavy and stiff, he waited. The one-sided conversation was hushed and short. When the phone clicked down, he was prepared to tell her a thing or two about the noise that kept him awake, the beer can flung in the street, but something in her face softened him, even made him say yes when she asked if they could park the van in his back yard, away from those heavy overhanging limbs.

Her look was warm, her movements unhurried. Borden asked if she would like a cup of coffee. Her eyes met his and held; her lips parted, "No, but I'll stay if you like." Borden said that wasn't what he meant, but she simply smiled and looked about, saying what a nice house he had, standing very close as he leaned against the doorjamb. Her hair had the fairness of clean yellow pine and smelled wonderfully fresh, skin evenly tanned and flawless, and her face was alert, knowing; it didn't have that cheerful vacancy he saw in the faces of college girls. But she might have been a few years older.

She followed him into the den. Again their eyes touched. She asked if he knew much about feet. Surprised, he looked at hers, in simple sandals, nicely shaped, the nails faintly painted, gray-blue. "Lie down on the sofa," she said. He laughed. She took his arm. "Trust me, I'll show you something." She explained in a steady voice that feet were the key to everything. As she untied his heavy work shoes, she talked about Reflexology. She had recently been on TV with a workshop group. Borden remembered: people sitting cross-legged on mats, playing with their bare feet. She winked. Her mouth said, "I usually charge, but you've been nice to let us stay in front of your house. Besides, I want more people to know about this." Borden was paralyzed, nostrils full of her scented closeness. She untied his other boot. Her eyes were the aquamarine you saw along the coast over sandy bottom when the sun was right. She explained how certain points in your feet control kidneys, neck, back, and so on. She worked the balls of his feet between her palms, one at a time, and then bent back his toes. "Feel good?"

Borden could only smile. She said there were many things about body and mind we were just beginning to discover. She knew a woman with great psychic powers. "While I do this," she said, "imagine a place, a place you actually know, or a place you would like to be. Close your eyes. Relax."

Borden nodded. He saw a wooden pier sticking out into the still water of the sound. As instructed, he added colors, sounds, smells.

Emerald eelgrass grew along the shore. An egret, dazzling white, stood one-footed on its own image, then moved forward, hunting, ducking its head out of sight. A school of jumping mullet roiled the glassy watertop, then leaped: brief silver sickles. A screen door slapped shut and Borden turned. A woman in a two-piece swimsuit, deeply tanned, came out on the porch and waved from the rail. It was Chrissy. Two older people—his parents!—came to the deck railing and waved. His father's glasses flashed in the sun; he stooped and lifted a little blond-haired boy in white shirt and shorts. They all laughed and waved from the deck of a house Borden knew he had built. The afternoon was everywhere gold, and a flotilla of small rosy clouds drifted south . . .

The van was gone.

That evening Borden stood by the front window. A green Camaro pulled into the slot where the van had been; a black guy got out and ambled toward his night class, doing one of those puppet walks. TV said the storm had moved up the coast and made landfall, causing moderate damage. Much of its strength was gone. Winds had dropped to fifty miles per hour. In fact, the National Weather Service had just downgraded Diana to "tropical storm" status. The moment was out of focus. Borden felt as empty as the street.

At the Steak n' Brew, he and Chrissy sat under wagon wheels with flame-shaped bulbs that hung on chains from a lowered ceiling. Cowgirls in yellow shirts, black leather vests, and tan ten-gallon hats brought trays of grilled steaks and foil-wrapped baked potatoes. Chrissy lifted her glass in celebration. "Today was your day."

"Our day," he said, and ordered another beer. The call from F. M. to report for work was a surprise, but not entirely, because he had overheard those old guys in Dodd Lumber talk about bids being out on a big complex of condos at West Island Harbor. A long job, plenty of O.T. Chrissy told about two people at the bank who were having an affair; the woman was her supervisor and took out her troubles on the other girls. Borden listened and thought about the girl from the van, how refreshed he had felt, utterly certain his fortunes would change. Her eyes were fathoms deep, sunny, blue.

He was working overtime every day now and often got home after dark. The street was quiet. Falling leaves fluttered in lamp-lit air. All the cars lining the far side of the street were compact and subcompact, almost uniform in size. They all pointed in the same direction, but that did not lift his mood. Something was slightly wrong. A coed on her way to night class stepped into the Datsun's beams, her face as pretty and vacant as a showgirl's. Borden thought of the trio on the promenade ("Bring it over here . . .") and of how long it had been since he and Chrissy . . .

Weary and stiff, he parked the truck, killed the lights, and sat in the dark. Though only weeks ago, it seemed, in memory, more like months, a year since he had seen the van.

Weekends, when occasionally he had Saturday off, he began working on the house, repairing this and that. He and Chrissy hung new wallpaper in the kitchen and bedroom. The spare bedroom they painted light blue. Finally, he faced the problem of seepage and began trenching the foundation. One October afternoon, taking a breather, leaning on his shovel, unaccountably, he found himself humming, then singing "Shenandoah." For a number of weeks, in the middle of the night, returning from the bathroom, he would pull the curtain aside and, peering down into the empty street, half expect to see the van, the palm trees and the swollen sun on its side.

Under the *Azure Dee*

"C'mon, get outta my face!"

"Give me the remote!"

Mark and Jennifer had been bickering on and off for an hour. Their voices, louder now, reached up the spiral stairs into the lookout room where Randall was peering through binoculars. He was watching a sloop a few hundred yards off shore. A slim woman with flying blonde hair and only a bikini bottom was hauling down the jib. Like a weathervane, the sloop pivoted on its anchor, and Randall read *Dora Lee* on the stern. Then he returned to the bruise-colored cumulus building on the horizon. He had just noticed the woman and the clouds. For a long time he had been simply staring out the window. He lifted the binoculars again just in time to see her slide under the boom and disappear below decks.

"Daddy!"

The cat jumped from Randall's desk. She had the coat of a Siamese but not the face, not the china blue eyes. Her ringed tail and legs were like comic pajamas. Randall tabled the binoculars and watched her stretch. "Gamine," he said, "that's a good idea," and stretched from side to side, then rotated his head. At forty-three, he had thick sandy hair, muscular tennis legs, and wore white Docker shorts and a green polo shirt. He twisted down the narrow metal stairs into a darkened living room. "Why the drawn drapes?"

"Darkness suits us," said Jennifer.

"Suits you, ditso," said Mark, "Not me."

"You're as mean as Daddy."

Randall said, "Why is somebody so upset?"

Jennifer was fourteen. Thin and pale, she wore an extra-large Nirvana T-shirt and had long dark hair. "Somebody's upset because somebody's so selfish. *Wuthering Heights* is on the movie channel, and that's on my summer reading list."

"Mmm, there should be a solution to this."

"Mmm, well, yes, naturally," mocked Jennifer. "Christ, I'm not one of your clients looking for a loan. Nothing bothers you two. Just alike."

"Jennifer, please?"

Mark said, "She's wigged because I'm watching World Cup." Well tanned, Mark was in surfer trunks, shirtless, and sprawled on the aqua-colored modular sofa with his Braves cap backwards.

"I should wash my hands of both of you," she said.

"Your brother will be leaving for college in two months, Jennifer. You'll have the TV all to yourself. We should try to help each other, not hurt each other."

She snorted. "Where's Gamine?"

"She's upstairs."

Mark said, "It's not like I don't have a special interest in this sport. It's paying my way to college, remember, ditso?"

"Duh, it's not like we don't get reminders." Jennifer flung herself onto the sofa, sitting with her knees drawn up under her chin. "Daddy, tell him not to call me that."

"Mark—"

"OK, Dad."

Into a lull, the sportscaster's voice erupted, grew wild, fans roaring.

"Baggio's fantastic," said Mark. "Man, it's like magic feet. Second goal in two minutes."

Jennifer put her forehead to her knees, hiding her face.

Catching Mark's eye, Randall said, "We might be feeling sorry for ourselves. Let's get out of these shadows and go for a walk on the beach."

Jennifer said, "I wish we never moved into this house. And don't say, 'Your mother would have wanted it.' I'm sick of that."

Randall drove over the bridge to Discovery Divers and pulled into a spot next to the dock. The largest dive boat, the *Azure Dee,* was gone, out on a charter. Kids were jumping off and splashing around a yacht at anchor. Randall walked over crushed shells to the shop.

Janet was using a pole with a hook to hang a Darlexx wet suit from the rafter above a display of Scubapro regulators, masks, and fins. Before she noticed Randall, a guy clapped him on the back and said, "Hey, way you been, man?"

"Oh, around," said Randall.

It was Itchy. Randall couldn't remember his real name. He was bulky from weights and had a mustache that swept from lips to jowls. He was in the diving course Randall and Mark had taken from Janet almost a year ago.

"Around? Hey, Janet, would you believe it? Randy says he's been around."

Behind Itchy, Janet gave Randall a great knowing wink. "Oh, I'll bet he has," she said.

"So what have *you* been up to?"

"Little as possible," said Itchy. He gave Janet a kind of leer as she moved off to help a customer. Lowering his voice, he said, "I'm not buying anything else in here, I'll tell you that. Vic never has sales. He's tight, tight as a crab's ass, and that's water-tight. See what I'm saying?"

Randall laughed. Since her divorce, Janet had been making new friends. Maybe Itchy was the latest. When Janet came back, he said, "Wha' say we grab us some lunch over at the Dock House?"

"Good idea," said Janet.

"Randy, we gone lighten you up. Look, I'll meet y'all. I got me a few calls to make."

Watching Itchy leave, Janet rolled her eyes, then smiled at Randall. "I've got some good news."

"What?"

"Be patient. Let me get my purse."

They sat under a candy-striped awning on the upper verandah of the Dock House. Across the channel, eelgrass fringing the island was vivid green. A school of menhaden dimpled far-side shallows. Janet studied his face and gave him a wink. "So, how's the weather?"

Randall grinned. "Well, I think I believe in God."

"Good, eight months ago you didn't."

"Well, I prayed Itchy wouldn't show, and it appears my prayers have been answered."

Janet said, "Poor Itchy."

"Poor! How so?"

"He's living some kind of fantasy."

"Well, everybody has some kind of fantasy. You're mine. That's why the thought of you getting tight with—"

"Yeah, right!"

"At the shop, he was checking you out, smacking his lips. Actually, I can't blame him. You're looking pretty good."

"Thanks, we do our best." Janet had round green eyes. The

bones of her cheeks were high, and when she smiled, fine spokes appeared around eyes that always seemed interested. She was thirty-one, trim, with short dark hair and a swimmer's sculpted shoulders.

"So what's this good news?" Randall asked.

"Well, Vic bought another boat, an old oil rig shuttle that he's had refitted for diving. He's opening up a new dive shop. And, tra-la, he wants me to manage it, hire a skipper, dive instructors, the whole nine yards."

"Great!"

Their waiter, a university student in deck shoes and safari shorts, set down utensils wrapped in a cloth napkin, a basket of hush puppies, and two tall glasses of iced tea with lemon slices.

Randall said, "So where's the new shop going to be?"

"South Carolina, Charleston."

"Charleston! Whoa, right through the heart. I thought you said *good* news."

"It is."

Randall looked at the island and shook his head. "For *you*. Why have I been thinking *us* for the last few months?" Across the channel, three of the island's wild horses topped the tallest dune, slowly moved downward into cedar shadows, hit the sun again, and followed each other westward along a narrow ridge of hard sand.

"It's not like it's going to be easy to leave," Janet said. "But it's an opportunity for me to be a free agent. With my ex, I was a nothing."

The breeze shifted and he could smell her hair, a faint scent of shampoo. She tilted her head, and the sun made the thin partition between her nostrils rosy, her skin a pliant bronze.

"Do I make you feel like nothing?"

"That's not the point," she said.

"It is if I've been good for you."

She squinted, watching the horses. "It's possible we've been conveniently using each other."

Randall breathed through his nose, then slapped the table. "Well, I guess I don't believe in God any more."

She laughed. "You're in much better shape now."

"Have you said yes to Vic?"

"Not yet." She reached over, adjusted his collar.

"Why are you doing this?" he asked.

"I just told you," she said. "It's something I have to do."

"I thought we had some kind of dibs on each other."

Janet laughed. "Be careful, you don't want to break down and use the L-word, do you?"

"Anything you want."

"You know, this is the first time we've been in public in this town. It's always been at night aboard the *Dee*, or in one of those empty houses you appraise for the bank. Dinner in some out-of-the-way place."

Randall said, "Come on. It's too soon for my kids. You know that. Especially Jennifer. Maybe even Mark. He still goes to the cemetery by himself sometimes. Jenny still hasn't put back the weight. And she thinks that because I've kept my tears to myself, kept working, and haven't seen a shrink, I'm some kind of monster. She's precocious, she's—"

"She's almost fifteen, Randy. Don't you think this very bright girl can understand her father might have needs that involve another woman?"

Randall began to laugh. "*Needs*, I like that. Let's steer clear of that L-word. We might wind up saying something we'd be sorry for."

A Bermudan ketch with no protruding wheelhouse or hatch covers chugged up the waterway for the open sea, its brightwork catching the sun.

"Beautiful, isn't it?" Janet said. "All the teak handrails and hatch covers really give it class."

"She could weather some rough seas too," Randall said. "You want to buy one?" He winked. "I could arrange a loan."

She chanted, "People at the bank'll figure it out."

"I'm sure people at the bank already have. This is a small town. Tell me something."

"Shoot."

"Is it this new opportunity, or are you just bored with me?"

A guy in scuffy work shoes and dusty Levis, a hammer sheath on his hip, came out of the bar. He stopped at the table. "Hey, how's it going?"

"Pretty good," said Randall. "How's business?"

"Great. Got more work than I can handle."

"This is Janet, a friend of mine."

"Hey."

After he left, Janet said, "Who was that?"

"Guy named Borden. A couple years ago, he was at the end of his string. We made him a loan to start a building and remodeling business."

Janet laughed. "In one day, we've gone from sneak around to meeting the public. That's progress."

"You not leaving would be the only progress I care about."

"Don't," she said, and looked out at the island again. "OK? I don't know, I'm afraid we might be clutching at straws."

Horses, one after another, their wind-lifted manes like fire, disappeared around the natural curve of the shore.

Randall drove over the high bridge, an archipelago of eelgrass islands strung out below. When he got back home, the Wrangler was gone.

"Jennifer?"

The house was empty. He took a beer from the refrigerator and climbed to the lookout room. The *Dora Lee* was gone. He stood and watched purple-black thunderheads on the southern horizon. There was something attractive and frightening about the sea-scape's simplicity. Footsteps rang on the metal stairs. "Hey, Dad."

"Where's Jennifer?"

"She was with me. I took her looking for the cat. You must have let Gamine out."

"Did I? God, I probably did."

"Jen went gaga. I said she wouldn't go anywhere but, no, we had to drive over to the old neighborhood. Then we see the house, and Jen starts crying because the new owners have let Mom's rose bushes go to pot." Mark began peering through the binoculars. "What a lightshow out there!" After a few moments, he put them down. "We get back here and Gamine, of course, is sitting on the front stairs."

Randall put his arm around Mark, squeezed his shoulder.

Jennifer sat on the sofa with the cat in her lap, brushing its fur, making a pile of whitish sheddings on the aqua cushion. Randall said, "Jen, there's a great lightshow out at sea."

"We don't want to look out, do we, Gamine? It's just the abyss with a bunch of strobes."

Randall smiled. "Hey, maybe Gamine likes looking out and doesn't like you making decisions for her. Besides, she used to be an outside cat."

"She's been strange ever since we moved here."

"Cats are paid to be strange," said Randall. "It's their *métier*. And all the sand around here—it's downright cruel to deprive her of such a great litter box."

Jennifer put a pretend mike to her mouth. "Thank you, thank you. . . . Our next guest here at the Comedy Store is—"

"Jennifer, do you want me to stop trying? Is that what you want?"

When the phone rang, Gamine sprang to the floor and Jennifer went into the kitchen. Randall stood there watching the cat clean herself. She licked each paw and repeatedly dragged it behind her ears. Then she yawned hugely and moved toward the spiral stairs. Jennifer came back and said in a loud, actressy way, "It's for you, Dad. It's your *paramour!*"

Randall grabbed her arm and squeezed. "You damned little—"

"Go ahead, say it," she screamed. "Say it, say it!"

He dropped her arm, took a deep breath, and went to the kitchen.

It was Janet. He closed the door and said, "Let me guess. You've changed your mind about South Carolina."

"Not quite. How's Jennifer treating you?"

"Topic of the day."

"She was very polite. I invited her to a dive party excursion on the Fourth of July. Vic's decided to pop for a trip, free air tanks and everything, then a pig pickin' at the shop when we get back to port. Preferred customers only."

"I appreciate it, but—"

"But what?"

"Mark'll be delighted, but I don't know about Jen."

"She can snorkel, can't she?"

Randall said she could.

"Well, we're diving on a freighter wreck, the *Indra*, where the wheelhouse and upper deck are only about fifteen feet down, so she'll be able to see all kinds of fish from the surface."

"I'll work on it."

"Let me give you one word, just one word, OK?"

"Go."

"Patience."

"I'll try," he said. There was a close sizzle of lightning and a great thunderclap rattling the kitchen windows. The phone filled with static.

"Randy, you still there?"

"Yeah, it's starting to storm. Look, before we get cut off, I'm wondering if you'd like to have lunch day after tomorrow? I also have to, ahem, appraise a house up around Marrow's Landing."

"Sounds like a setup."

"Well, according to the marine weather report, this front's going to be squatting over us for the next two days. No charters, you'll just be stuck in the shop."

"This sounds kind of like a serious date."

"I thought you enjoyed looking at old houses. I don't know, maybe it's not a good idea."

"Wait, wait. I didn't hear myself say no. Will you put a rose between your teeth?"

"I might."

"How long will we be gone?"

"I don't know—fifteen, twenty years."

When Randall walked out of the kitchen, Jennifer said, "You're a goddamned phony, Dad, a complete fake."

Mark drove, and Randall sat in the back. Jennifer controlled the radio, stopped on "Midnight Train to Georgia," then switched stations.

Randall said, "Jen, I happen to like that song. It's a classic."

"Well, I don't, and whoever sits up here controls the radio, remember? Family ordinance number 1632."

They rolled past a blue tent between two steep banks of sand. A boy stood next to his mother, who seemed to be tending smoke at a camp stove. A man in a sleeveless T-shirt emerged from the tent.

"Where are we going anyway?" asked Jennifer.

"Just killing time," said Randall. "Our reservation isn't until eight o'clock. We used to camp down here before you were born."

"We better not be going to The Flying Bridge."

"Why?" asked Mark.

"That was Mom's favorite place," said Jennifer. "You shouldn't even have to ask."

"This was also her favorite town," said Mark. "Maybe we should move to Piss Hole, West Virginia."

"That's enough," said Randall.

The one-lane road was partly sanded over and finally came to an end. On the left, there was a rusted fence that ran down to a stone breakwater and a channel full of swirling eddies. A sweep of dunes lay in smooth curves on the right. Randall told Mark to shut off the motor. He told them about the dive excursion on the Fourth of July.

"All right!" said Mark.

Randall said, "Jen, I have a favor to ask."

"Dad, I'm not much for that kind of thing."

Mark said to Jennifer, "Hey, haven't I been your private chauffeur? Did I ever say no when you needed a ride somewheres?"

"Where, not wheres."

Randall said, "I forget her first name, but the Wilson girl will be there. And probably some other kids you know."

Jennifer looked straight ahead.

Randall said, "Here's something else to think about. You'll still be on the newspaper this fall, won't you?"

Jennifer unfolded her arms and nodded.

"Well, the skipper/divemaster of the *Azure Dee* is an interesting guy. You could shoot some pictures with the Minolta, interview him, and have your first feature written before school even starts."

Mark said, "C'mon, Jen."

A line of pelicans, hedge-clippers with wings, straggled past and, one after another, crashed into the waterway with big white splashes. Jennifer said, "I'm hungry, let's go."

They were still in protected water before crossing the bar. Randall and Jennifer climbed up to the wheelhouse. "Come on in," said Ken, the skipper. He was drinking coffee from a slosh-proof mug and eating a banana. From its basket on the dash, a fat black cat, white chin and paws, looked at them with drowsy green eyes.

Randall said, "Ken, this is my daughter, Jennifer."

"Hey there, darlin." Close to sixty, his face was seamed and tanned, and he kept tugging on the pulpy tip of his nose. There was a bit of swagger about him, somebody who prided himself on being one of a kind. He had an anchor tattoo on the back of his hand.

"Hi, can I pet him?" asked Jennifer.

"Sure, scratch his ears, you'll be friends forever."

"Doesn't he get seasick?" asked Jennifer.

"Popeye? Nah, cats adjust to anything. Besides, he'd rather be with me than in an empty house. Divers always spear a fish for him, that I cook at night."

Jennifer asked the captain if she could interview him for her school newspaper.

"Sure, fire away."

"How long have you been doing this?"

Dusting the tip of his nose with a thick forefinger, Ken told her he was career Navy until he retired. Then a police diver, car wrecks, the recovery of drowning victims, that sort of thing. But he'd also been skipper of a patrol boat in Vietnam. Randall left when Ken was explaining the CRT depth recorder and how it color-sketched a profile of reefs and wrecks, how it could zoom in for particulars.

The bones of Randall's feet tingled from the vibration of the steel deck. The boat plunged, spray came over the bow, and teenagers up front yelled. Mark was there with two of his friends. A big offshore Scarab roared past on the starboard, catching lots of air under its red hull. A pair of T-shirts and sunglasses gave them the wave. An attractive woman with long dark hair was between them.

"What talent, huh?"

It was Itchy. Randall nodded. Itchy kept changing the position of the huge dive knife strapped to his ankle.

"Two on one—interesting possibilities." When Randall said nothing and looked away, Itchy said, "I mean, what's all this waving on the water? People in cars don't wave. I reckon if you was going under, they'd probably keep right on going. See what I'm saying?"

Randall wanted to disagree, but Itchy said "Ouch" when one of the high school girls came from below decks in a one-piece swimsuit, blue and white. "Women," said Itchy, and began telling him about a friend who, on days off, with much frustration, taught his wife how to drive. "So finally she gets her license and . . ."

Half listening, Randall watched the southeast darken to an angry purple. In the middle distance was a pool of sunlight that came and went as the bow rose and fell.

Itchy said, "So guess what happens?"

Coming back, Randall shrugged.

"One day she don't pick him up, OK? So he's walking home, pissed off, and here she comes, drives right past, smiling and waving bye-bye, the car full of her stuff." Itchy laughed and repeated the punch line, "Bye, bye!" Again, he adjusted the dive knife strapped to his ankle. "He teaches her how to drive, she leaves him, in *his* car!" Squinting toward the horizon, he shook his head. "Who can figure it out?"

The *Azure Dee* plunged and spray flew. Janet staggered by and told them not to worry.

"Who's worrying?" said Itchy, yanking the knife out of its black sheath and sticking the blade, pirate-style, between his teeth.

Janet said, "It'll flatten out at the wreck."

Randall watched her go aft where one of the shop instructors was testing a regulator. The boat pitched and Janet leaned her body into the instructor's, knocking her head into his chest. They laughed.

"Looks like more than friends," said Randall.

"That's a negatory," said Itchy. "There's only one man she cares about."

"Really?"

"You ought to know," he said.

Everyone was suited in rental black and looked like members of some strange cortège. Weight belt on, Randall helped Mark hoist and get into his yellow tank and vest. There were loud blasts of air from divers checking regulators. Diesel smoke blew into their faces from the stern. "Mark, check my tank valve."

Reaching up, Mark said, "You're fine, Dad," and moved heavily off to the railing.

"That smoke is making me sick."

Janet said, "One of our divers is down setting the anchor. It'll be just a minute. Loosen your vest a bit."

The diver surfaced and yelled, "Great viz. At least sixty feet!"

The engines stopped, gave way to an eerie quiet. The surface without sun was black.

Randall said, "I've decided not to try to change your mind."

"I don't know what to say," Janet said.

"You already said it last week, that rainy day at Marrow's Landing."

She smiled. "What did I say?"

"Charleston isn't that far."

"Well, I meant it."

"I know, that's why I've got religion again," he said, forcing a smile. "No matter what, though, you've helped me a lot, more than I've—"

Janet put her hand to his mouth.

Randall laughed. "OK, OK, I'm nervous though. I haven't done a dive in a long time."

"I'll partner with you."

Randall said, "Thanks for inviting the Wilson girl."

Janet winked. "Never mind. Just remember, how you go under is very important. One thing at a time. Ease the air out of your vest until you start sinking down the anchor line. As soon as you feel pressure in your ears, equalize, pinch your nose. Don't worry, I'll be right there."

Mark, with one hand on his mask and the other on the bottom of his tank, turned, took a giant step, and popped up in the dissolving white of his splash. With clipboard and watch, Ken recorded the number and time of entry of each diver. He told Randall he'd keep an eye on Jennifer and her friend.

Randall thanked him, then said to Janet, "I don't know. My stomach—"

"Don't worry. You'll feel better as soon as we get under," she said, pulling her mask into place.

She was right. Link after link, he lowered himself down the anchor chain into the world of waver and slide. A stream of bubbles from divers below grew in size and wobbled upward past his face. Janet's round green eyes looked at him from behind her mask, asking for an OK. He made the standard thumb and forefinger circle. She pinched her nose, reminding him to equalize, which he did, and the pain left his ears with a pop. Then things came into greater focus. Mark had buddied with Itchy, and together they moved away in a graceful slo-mo across the deck.

Reluctantly letting go of the anchor chain, Randall drifted over the horns of a mooring cleat, bright orange, made asymmetrical by a sea urchin stuck to one of its tips. Antlers of yellow coral spiked up from the great garden of rust. Janet pointed to a tiny blue wrasse, bright as a drop of wet ink, hiding in the coral. Randall extended his finger, and it moved out of reach. He breathed slowly, calmly. Clutches of pink tubeworms, like asters, swayed in the underwater wind, opening and closing. In front of them, a huge billow of silversides flashed as they moved from right to left, turning precisely, as if they were scales on the flank of a single great fish, the act of each mysteriously integrated within the larger ballet of the school, a shape in continuous change.

Janet was there. He could feel her presence without looking. Slowly, he finned forward. He was weightless now, held warmly by water, his breathing steady and slow. Above the dark yawn of a deck hatch, a great grouper hovered, then sank out of sight, as if in a dream where there is nothing to fear.

Filling the Igloo

Surf, gulls, and a long stretch of empty sand—Jack Quinn has this all to himself. Leaning back in a low sand chair, legs stretched, he takes a sip of beer and sets the can on the lid of a red and white Igloo. With binoculars, he scans a tall pier that juts well past the surf into the ocean; figures are hunched at the rail behind a crazy web of sunlit monofilament. In less than a minute five or six fish catch the sun in the long space between water and rail. Glittering like confetti, gulls work a baitfish school just off the end of the pier. Quinn rubs his eyes and checks his rod, held by a sand spike, the tip barely stirring. "Damn! All the action's out there."

Hoisting the binoculars again, he looks in the other direction: two fishermen waist-deep in the surf, small with distance. And three other figures: his wife, Joni, her brother—Gerald's bow-legged gait is unmistakable—and Jimmy. "Shit." Quinn takes a deep breath, looks at his watch and times their arrival.

Little Jimmy says, "Dad, whatja get?"

Joni says, "Why not fish in front of the cottage?"

Quinn says, "Too many kids and bathers."

Gerald says, "Don't worry, we won't disturb you." He has hidden his gray hair with black dye and wears an orange bikini brief. He moves off toward the dunes.

Quinn says, "What's with him? Didn't he have his morning joint yet?"

"Be nice, Jack."

"What's with that bikini? If I wore something like that, he'd mock me."

Joni says, "He bought it when he played that concert in France last year. It's the style on the Riviera."

"Well, this isn't the Riviera. But I could name an island in New York where they wear those things."

"Dad, didja get anything?"

"Jack, be kind."

"Why? He's always pushing my buttons."

"My brother is depressed."

"Dad, you get anything?"

"No, but I'm not depressed."

"Uncle Gerald!" The boy runs off.

"You don't have to be sarcastic in front of Jimmy."

"Sarcasm is something I learned from your brother."

Joni folds her arms, tightens her lips.

"I'm sorry," says Quinn, "but your brother's not going to ruin my vacation."

"He might go back to the city tomorrow."

Quinn shakes his head. "Why?"

"He says that the ocean overwhelms him."

"It's supposed to."

"Well, he can't practice here."

"The temperamental artist bit. What about Denise and the boys?"

"They'll stay. Jack, don't be a prick."

Lifting the binoculars and looking toward the pier, Quinn says, "Listen, he's addicted to an image he created years ago. I'm not supporting his habit, that's all. It's always got to be some kind of melodrama with him." Off the tip of the pier there is a charter boat; the stern reads: "Time Out." Two fish on a single bottom rig flash as they flip over the gunwale.

In the pier parking lot, crowded with pickups, vans, and RVs, a thin man in tan work pants and shirt is lifting a cooler onto the tailgate of his pickup. "Any luck?" Quinn asks.

"Yup, lotta action this morning." The guy opens a green Coleman cooler, all fisheye and slither, sad mouths and bloody gills.

"Good size. What are they?"

"Spanish."

And the man is gone. Quinn squints into the distance at a telephone pole in the heat waves: a snake stood on end.

The only access is through a long paintless shack that tilts drunkenly to one side; tattered curtains swim from open windows at the rear. Inside, he leans his new Diawa and Garcia combo against the counter. Reels, rods, and nets hang from the ceiling. Quinn looks at the trophies—an arching tarpon with big scales, leaping Spanish and king mackerel, blue fish, black drum, sheepshead, and others—all identified by hand-scrawled cards. And strategically placed, another sign: "All Fish Caught On This Pier." There is an old woman in black with one tooth like the prong of a can opener. Quinn says he wants a ticket to fish. She says nothing. He asks how much it is. She lets the register answer with a ding and a readable $5.00. And what are they catching the Spanish on? Wide-hipped, rump like an ottoman, she shuffles in pink fluffy slippers, reaches down a cellophane packet, skates back, and drops it on the counter. "A jerk-jigger, hunh?"

The register speaks again: $3.40.

Outside on the pier a sign says "No Shark Fishing." A guy in rolled-up Levis, his nipples trapped in a net jersey, strides for the scale suspended near the water-sluiced cleaning tables; he is carrying a fish that is easily a yard long. He hooks it by the bright bloody gills and when the pointer stops quivering at twenty-eight pounds, there are long moans of envy. He drifts back down the pier in an actorish way, basking in his own private sunshine, wearing the look of someone who has just proved something. "Spanish mackerel's the same thang, jes' smaller," a father is telling his son. "But you gotta cas' fo' um."

Most of the casting takes place on the last third of the pier, and Quinn begins to make his way to where the action is. A sand shark buzzes with flies on the salt-bleached planks. Teenage boys fish to the beat of a boom-box; the number is "Bad Moon Rising." The pier seems to gather all kinds: old and young blacks, a fat white woman whose head is hived with pink curlers, a jabbering Japanese family, a crew-cut Marine with a white sun-blocked nose. "Some crew," whispers Quinn. They are merely bottom fishing, content with spots, blues, an occasional mullet or flounder. Quinn follows two laughing girls; their liquid brown bodies are beautifully packed into shorts and halters that bounce and sloop with each step as they follow the net-shirted guy with the mackerel.

There. Quinn will have about five feet of railing to himself. He stoops to his tackle box. The lure has a brand name; it is called "Gotcha"—a three-inch white plastic tube with a red Day-Glo tip, a treble hook fore and aft. One of his rail-mates, an old man with skin as brown as a penny, tells Quinn not to use leader. "Spanish kin spot it. Cut off the front hook. You won't foul, git better action."

Quinn gets out his pliers. "Like this?"

"Dash rat." The old guy looks at him. "You been here long?"

Quinn shakes his head. "Yesterday."

"Where you fum?"

"Ohio."

"Like it heah?"

"I'm working on it."

He laughs. "Pier ain't spose to be work."

The sky and a few thin horsetail clouds are red with the lower-ing sun—the same red as the skin on Quinn's neck, legs, and arms. Suddenly the old man's rod becomes a drawn bow, the drag singing. The rod jerks and trembles. He reels in, tightens the drag. The monofilament, brightly beaded, shears the water nicely. The old man talks as he plays the fish: "You wont to keep it away fum the spiles. No hurry. You can snap the line . . ." The drag no longer clicks, and the mackerel's flanks flash in the green as it comes to the surface. "Two-three pounds," says the old man. "No need to lower no gaff or net." Over the railing it comes, flips on the planks. Quinn looks closely. "Spanish mackerel," he whispers. Iridescent blue along the dorsal, gray-silver flanks stippled with light gold. Pretty as ice-bedded trout in the ads. The old-timer points his chin off to the right. "See um jump?" At first Quinn doesn't, then yes, far off, lots of small arcs and splashes. A school. And the pier is a flurry of movement, yells.

There. Somebody further down the pier is swinging in anoth-er. Quinn is all thumbs with the knots. The plug is light and doesn't fly far. The next cast is better. In the clear water, two mack-erel follow the lure, then swerve off at the last second. "Shit!" He blows the next cast. But this time the plug flies in a long arc, plops under, and begins to work—a great pull and the line is alive, the drag whining. The old-timer tells him not to tighten down yet. Quinn keeps it away from the pilings, the other lines, a nice three-pounder that, as it leaves the water, snaps the line with a great last flutter.

"Get you a jerk jigger fum mah box," says the old guy.

With one knee on the planks, Quinn takes no time to chat with these two tourist girls asking questions.

Then, as he is about to stand up, there is a quick, sharp pain at

the corner of his eye. His face snaps around in the wrong direction; it leans, stretches, and tries to lessen its pain. He loses his bal-
ance and sits, then gets to his knees. He yells, wraps the line
around his fist to keep the boy from pulling. Blood is dripping
from his jaw, channeling down his neck. The boy's face is as white
as his sun-bleached hair, the mouth slack. "Easy nah," says the father, a man with a belly that flabs over belted green trousers. A
baseball cap shades his upper face; the teeth are crooked and
stained with nicotine. "Boy here . . . forgit . . . look out." He speaks
slowly, his voice such a twisted drawl that Quinn can barely catch
a word of what he says. "Nah didja, boy?"

"No suh," says the boy. Tears brim.

To Quinn, the father says, "Holt stee-yul" and cuts the line at
the plug. Other faces drift back to their stations; a few stay. "Hit's
gone through the skin twicet" says a voice with a black cowboy
hat. The father just stands there, a dead cigarette dangling from
his dry, discolored lips. He keeps slapping a Zippo lighter against
his thigh, trying the wheel again, hands cupped at the cigarette tip.
Quinn dabs his handkerchief about the corner of his eye but the
plug is in the way and as long as the hook stays in, it will bleed,
leak into his eye if he fails to keep it closed.

"Let me look, I'm a doctor."

The voice belongs to a tuna-shaped man in a yellow sport shirt
with blue and red sailboats on it. No, it can't be pulled back
through because of the barbs: too much tearing. He speaks with
a pipe clamped in the side of his mouth. Even when the doctor
touches the plug lightly, Quinn pulls back. He instructs the father
to disassemble Quinn's rod. Which the man does, then resumes
work on the Zippo. Finally the doctor is ready; he will cut the
barbs with pliers and simply slide out the smooth shank.

"But, ah, Burt dear, you, ah . . ." This voice comes from a
woman in a tennis dress; she has frosted hair, and she shakes a

plastic glass with ice cubes and a green olive. A shadow crosses the doctor's face. He chortles nervously. "Well, actually I'm a dentist," he says. "I might get in trouble for this. Better let an M.D. take care of it. I'm, ah, I'm just on vacation here." And he describes in great detail the people he is with and the location of their cottage, "The Xanadu." There is a pause and the father speaks, blowing into the Zippo and tapping it as if it were a mike; he says there is a doctor on the other end of the island, Pantigo Inlet. "On the lay-ff, pas' the water tower, only house on the point." The dentist relents, decides he can at least tape Quinn's handkerchief to his cheek in such a way as to keep things from getting too messy. "That M.D.'ll fix you right up. Besides you're going to need a tetanus shot."

Quinn grabs the empty Igloo, tackle box, and rods.

The boy says he is real sorry.

The father offers to drive him to the doctor's place. Quinn shakes his head and flinches, a runnel of blood sliding onto his cheek.

In the parking lot, a trio of young men are unloading a pickup with a camper top. One of them asks Quinn about the action on the pier, then notices the jerk-jigger dangling from the corner of his eye. "By gawd, yew got chew a big un!" And they all laugh.

Fucking rednecks. Quinn speeds beneath the looming, four-legged water tower that rises in the windshield like a childhood giant. The road forks. He can't remember if the guy said left or right. "Fuck it—left for luck." This has to be Pantigo Inlet Road. A house by itself at the point: faded green shingles, peeling storm shutters, and a wrap-around deck. Quinn crunches to a stop on the white shell-paved road. Salt-stunted palmettos rattle their mocking fronds in the wind. There is a sign on a wooden yard-arm: "Percy Bynum, M.D."

Quinn sits on a high stool.

Blood drips from his jaw, and his hair is plastered with sweat. He stares at the floor, listens to the click of a cabinet door, the plink of a metal container, the rip of paper, the hiss of a faucet. The doctor, small and fiftyish and gray, adjusts a gooseneck lamp, rips open a hermetic bag of suture materials and places them on the towel-covered table next to him. Quinn winces as the doctor squirts a cleaning solution on the wound and snorts, "Don't get me started on that pier. Do you know what this is?" He holds up a pair of stainless steel pliers, his accent northern, maybe Boston. "Isn't a week goes by I don't use them to cut a hook." Quinn sees himself in the cabinet window. The jerk-jigger dangles from the skin at the corner of his eye and creates a Chinese effect. It looks like a drunken attempt at self-adornment. The doctor says, "Don't move now." He holds up a syringe. "This is a local."

Quinn feels a thin prick. The doctor's face leans close. Two patches of stubble where the razor has missed. A dab of dried shaving cream behind the ear. The lips are cracked and the corners of the wide mouth hook down and betray impatience. Quinn winces at the second prick.

"Give it a minute." He shakes his head, sighs wearily.

"Do you live here all year round?" Quinn asks.

The doctor nods yes.

"What's it like?"

"Quiet is what it's like . . . most of the time," he says, no relish in his voice, and looks at his shoes, brown penny loafers.

"How does somebody come out here to live anyway?"

The doctor's irises disappear, the gray hardens. "Dozens of reasons." His voice has an edge and his jaw muscles bunch when he pauses. "You inherit property, you think you like the quiet life, boats, fishing. Your wife runs off, kids grow up. Signs of angina. Dozens of reasons." He taps the skin around the wound. "Feel this?"

Quinn says no.

"Don't move," says the doctor. There is a loud snap and the lure clanks into a stainless steel basin. "There." After irrigating the wound, he very quickly takes three stitches as if he is anxious to see Quinn gone. Then he gives him a tetanus shot with directions to have his own doctor remove the stitches in a week or so. The doctor walks with him out to the verandah and tells him how once he saw someone lose an eye on the pier, come into the office with it hanging from the socket like a loose button. "You're lucky," he says, "very lucky."

His son, Jimmy, and his nephews, Julian and Larry, crowd close to the sink board where Quinn stands with two Spanish mackerel on an opened newspaper.

Joni says, "They've just been hanging around, bored."

"Sure they're bored—no TV or video games."

"Jesus, Jack."

"Christ, how could they possibly be bored? There's an ocean they never see fifty feet out the back door."

The boys, all wearing baseball hats and numbered jerseys, brush against his legs.

"Dad?"

"What?"

"What are you doing?"

"Sharpening my fishing knife."

"What are you going to do, Uncle Jack?"

"Cut the head off. Like . . . so, and gut it."

Gerald, changed from his bikini and sipping a beer, gives up a stoned giggle.

"Ah, gross!" says Julian.

"Sick."

"Really!"

Gerald says, "You probably *bought* them."

"Not true," says Quinn, stung by the accuracy of Gerald's guess. "I got these before—"

"Before that redneck kid hooked the big one?"

Quinn says, "Is everybody who doesn't know Mozart a redneck?"

"Tell the boys about some of your adventures as a captain on that tuna boat—the, ah, *Chicken of the Sea,* wasn't it?"

"Right."

"Down around the Bermuda Triangle, wasn't it?"

Quinn taps the knife on the counter and levels a cold look.

Gerald sighs, "Ah yes, Captain Quinn. But that was—hell, Ahab was still just a gleam in his father's eye."

Quinn says nothing.

Gerald has neatly styled hair, Italian glasses with small tinted lenses. Quinn watches him and his wife, Denise, from the kitchen; they are out on the deck now with cups of coffee, the ocean going a deeper green with evening. Quinn sees that Gerald is hollow in the cheeks. His skin should be glowing, but it's not. Joni finishes drying the last of the dinner dishes and says, "Christ, you could have lost an eye."

Quinn takes a last mouthful of coffee and puts his cup in the sink.

"Jack, taking off by yourself is—"

"Is the same thing we do when we ski at Snowbird—"

"'Everyone does their own thing,'" she mocks.

"Hey, I wanted us to have fish."

"We can buy fish."

"That's failure. It's what your brother would do. Not me."

After a few minutes, she says, "Are you going to take the boys fishing?"

"If I don't, nobody else will."

"Jack, be fair. Gerald's a musician. He wouldn't know a rod from—"

"A dish towel? He could help in the kitchen, you know."

"Jack, I don't mind." She says it plaintively.

"Well, *I* do. Why did they come? They could read novels in New York."

"We're family, remember? Why not forget the pier for tonight? We'll have some drinks and play board games with the children."

Quinn says, "Sorry. Whatever might save this friggin' day isn't here."

Gerald and Denise come off the deck into the living room and light cigarettes. Quinn doesn't smoke, and the Salem fog irritates his nostrils. Loud laughter comes through the wall from the other side of the duplex. He has only caught a glimpse of these other renters but doesn't like what he has seen: five cars in a space for two. This morning he had to knock on the door to ask them to move the car that blocked him in.

Gerald stretches out on the sofa, puts a pillow under his head and finds his place in *The Last Exit to Brooklyn*. He looks over his glasses at Quinn. "Off to the pier with the boys?"

"That's it."

"Why not stay? We could sit down and tell sad stories of the death of kings."

"Right," says Quinn.

"Well, break a leg."

"Thanks."

"Captain Quinn?"

"What?"

"Know what they say a pier really is?"

Quinn shakes his head.

"A disappointed bridge."

The boys are already in the Audi when Quinn steps onto the back porch. They are playing with the power locks, and the antenna goes up and down with an electric groan. They are bouncing, climbing on the seats. Quinn inhales deeply, thinks of Dr. Bynum. *Very lucky.*

It is dark when they roll into the parking lot. Quinn has stopped at Fishin' Fever for bait and a few different lures and now, damn it, he is ready for fish. At first the boys don't want to carry anything, but, by Christ, they will be responsible if he has anything to do about it. Julian lugs the Igloo, Jim carries the crab trap, Larry the tackle box.

The jukebox inside is blasting. The boys give a yeah of recognition and Jimmy, barely ten, begins to nod to the beat. The old woman in black is still there selling tickets, sandwiches. An old guy is dickering about a senior citizen discount. A small TV flickers behind the counter; it shows the news, a soldier with a rocket launcher, a building collapsing in a cloud of smoke and dust. When Quinn digs out his wallet and points to the children, the old woman points to a sign: "Children Under Twelve Admitted Free." Quinn says, "My lucky day." The woman in black looks at him blankly.

There are few spaces along the railing. A T-shirted fat man stares at him, then fishes in a baggie full of olive seaweed veined with bloodworms. "Bad Moon Rising" is blatting from a radio on a bench between two black boys holding rods and nodding their corn-rowed heads. Larry and Julian yell and kick at a dead sand shark on the planks. "Hey, Dad, look, a shark!"

"Gross me out!"

"Really!"

They have reached a point just past the breaking surf below them where everything is a field of white foam; now it deepens and darkens. Quinn hurries to a ten-foot segment of vacant rail. It is a choice location with a spotlight shining down into the water so you can see what you are doing. He begins rigging up, using the three rods, cooler, tackle box, and crab traps to stake out their territory against invasion. Slowly, one by one, each of the boys has a rod to hold. They yell, laugh, and keep jerking up their lines unnecessarily, letting them go slack. "Hey, look," says Julian, "There's a Ferris wheel." A half-mile down the beach a rotating white neon ring stands out against the dark; inside it is a green six-pointed star. There are other colored lights. A small carnival perhaps.

By the time Quinn has found some fish heads, baited the traps, and placed them near pilings on the other side of the pier, somebody is fishing on the fringe of his territory. The guy wears Levis and a black T-shirt from which his face rises like a moon. The T-shirt advertises Wild Turkey in white letters on the back.

"He's a turkey all right," mutters Quinn.

The guy has tangled lines with little Larry.

Two chesty teenage girls pause and move on; one of them says, "I guess it's her first love-type experience."

"Dad, can we go down to that carnival?"

"No!" says Quinn. "You wanted to fish, now *fish*."

The boys grumble.

A guy wearing a white sleeveless T-shirt, tall with a scraggly beard, a belly, and a hat saying Wayne Feeds, joins Wild Turkey. They are both using red-and-white bobbers. Shortly, both drags sing out and after a minute of loud reeling, two good-sized fish shiver over the rail and slap against the rough planks. Several other fishermen come over and say "Sea mullet."

"*Dad*," whines Jim, "how come we're not getting nothing?"

"Uncle Jack, is their bait same as ours?"

Quietly, Quinn says he doesn't know.

"Well, why don't we use the same thing?"

In a growl-whisper, he says, "Just shut up and fish. You don't even have your line tight."

"Gee-*wiz!*"

"Uncle, I'm going in to the bathroom, OK?"

Quinn says yes.

"Me too."

"Dad, can I have money for an ice cream?"

Quinn says no, they came to catch fish, not eat ice cream. The boys run down the pier, their footfalls like receding thunder. Quinn leans his rod against the rail and walks to the other side to check one of the crab traps. *Wild Turkey. Just like the jerks this afternoon. Wise-ass rednecks.* Quinn pulls his Rapalla knife from its leather and looks toward Wild Turkey. *You find another fishin place, man, or you're gonna be wearin your fucking guts for suspenders. Got it?*

"Hey, hey."

Quinn is squatting next to the trap, scooting out the hermit crabs. "Hey!" It's Wild Turkey. He holds Quinn's rod.

"You got one," says Wayne Feeds, his eyes glinting.

Wild Turkey says, "Rod was jumpin' like mad. Didn't want y'all to lose him, so I set the hook." He hands the rod to Quinn.

The line is alive, heavy with pull. The fish breaks water at the edge of the light pool: a silver flash. The wooden pier thunders when the boys, at a distance, see the fish flapping on the planks and come running. "Dad, Dad, what is it?"

"Wow!"

Quinn deepens his voice, "Quiet down, you guys."

"But, *Dad,* what is it?"

Jesus.

Wild Turkey says, "It's a sea mullet, boy."

"Tha's right," Wayne Feeds puts in. "Nice size."

Wild Turkey looks at Quinn and grins. "A day-um sight bigger in ours too."

"Right nice fish."

"Thanks," says Quinn and drops it into the cooler. His hands are slippery with slime. Just as he is ready to use his jeans, Wayne Feeds says, "Feels gewd, duden it?" and throws him a blood-spotted hand towel. They laugh.

Quinn has to say thanks again.

"You get 'im on bloodworms?"

"Dad, hey Dad?"

"That's right," says Quinn. "Bloodworms."

"Dad?"

A teenager walks by with a boom box: it's "Bad Moon Rising" once again.

"Dad!"

"What, for Chris'sake!"

"Can, can we go over to the carnival?"

"Yeah, can we, Uncle Jack?"

Quinn looks down at them. He sighs.

"We'll be real careful."

"Really," says Julian.

"We'll walk on the beach."

Quinn says, "Go, go." He waves his hand. "I give up."

"Dad?"

"What?"

"Can we have some money?"

Jesus.

"So?" It's Joni. She places her hand on Quinn's shoulder. Gerald keeps walking out to the end of the pier where the anchor rigs are, the shark and king lines; his white shirt begins to float in the dark, a ghost. "Where are the boys?"

"See that Ferris wheel?" says Quinn. "Don't look at me like that."

"Like what? Am I supposed to be cross?"

"They just can't sit still," he says.

"How's your eye? Still sensitive?"

"It's OK."

Joni laughs. "Mister Macho."

"Bag it, huh? Sounds like your brother."

Joni shakes her head. "You could spend some time with him."

"The only way for me to get along with Gerald is by *not* spending time with him. His ego is a black hole, and I'm not allowing myself to get sucked in."

"Jack—"

Quinn holds up his finger. "I want to show you something." He quickly opens the Igloo. "Look!"

"Nice. What are they?"

"Sea mullet."

"How do you know?"

"I just do. And I'm going to fill the Igloo too."

Two guys thump down the pier; they are laughing, and one keeps saying, "Take a break, take a break!"

Quinn says, "You like the pier?"

"It's pretty out here." Joni looks toward a trawler, a source of drifting gold light in the darkness.

Under his breath, Quinn says, "These people are something else. Half the time I can't make out—" He stops and studies the tip of his rod, clicking the line tighter. "Waves move the bait around."

"Jack, Gerald's going back."

Quinn jerks his rod to a vertical position, then gently tugs line in the porcelain eyelets.

Joni says, "He's sick and is afraid it's sarcoma."

Quinn settles back, still focused on his line. "That a disease or a New York fad?"

Joni crosses her arms and looks again toward the disappearing lights of the trawler.

"Come on," says Quinn, "I'm just kidding."

"It's nothing to kid about."

"No? What about the time he told you he was going blind?"

"This is different."

"Just a different ploy for attention. He's depressed, he's going blind, the ocean overwhelms him, he's got—whatever. Jesus, Joni. What's Denise doing?"

"I don't know."

"Maybe if she'd put down that novel once in a while . . ."

"The problem is deeper than that," says Joni.

But Quinn straightens on his bench, leans forward, and tries the line. Suddenly it tugs, pulls steadily. The drag buzzes and subsides; he begins to reel, peering into the dark for the first glimpse of what he has caught coming in. When he finally has the mullet in the Igloo, his eye begins to throb at the root. He looks around for Joni and sees her with Gerald, his white shirt floating, growing small with distance.

Six or seven halos of Coleman light are spaced along the beach to the south. A revolving green star in a white circle. Quinn watches a single light speeding along the beach, bouncing, followed by another: bikers. Hell, he wishes the boys had stayed. Tomorrow he can play ball with them on the low-tide sand. But Gerald—the only way to deal with him is not to. Clouds travel overhead. Stars seem to pulse. Or is it his eye? People up and down the pier mumble clichés about the weather and fishing, but their voices are wonderful. Behind him two teenage boys curse and continue to reel in an assortment of fish. Wild Turkey has left, and an old woman who has taken his spot at the rail turns and tells Quinn she has caught nothing all evening. She wears a wide-brimmed straw hat and has a narrow birdlike face. She looks at the cursing boys and back at Quinn: "Say in the Book it raineth on the just and the unjust alike."

Her husband says, "Amen."

She tells him they have a new preacher in their church, *needed* a new preacher. "I seen hogs house the devil."

Jesus. Quinn concentrates on his line. With two Spanish mackerel already in the refrigerator, the mullet he has caught and those Wild Turkey has given him, he has more than enough to feed the whole crew, but he can't leave, won't leave until he has filled the Igloo, even if it takes all night. Lights, glittering on the smooth dark water in the distance, look like sweepings of broken glass, a small neat pile. The old woman says something about Judgment. Quinn tightens his line. He is trying not to think about Gerald when a black man ten feet up the rail hauls in a big blue. Then someone else. And another and another. Finally his own line comes alive and all along the pier the darkness flashes with bluefish swinging from dozens of poles.

The Price of Dining Out

Julia stopped typing. She frowned at the laptop screen: *As owner and hostess of a restaurant pretending to class, you should look and act the part, not like some Jacksonville hooker, boob tattoo, plum lips, and enough mascara to be taken for a raccoon—*

"Julia! Come here, *quick!*"

She darkened the screen and got to the kitchen just in time to see a small colorful blur at the window.

Chad laughed. "Sorry, hon, you need quicker feet."

Julia said, "And there goes my train of thought."

Chad said, "This white millet's like a magnet. They love it."

She looked at the empty pegs of the feeder swaying in the on-shore breeze, then watched a catamaran with purple sails making its way seaward down Bogue Sound. Summer was on the fly. Julia taught at a small Methodist college and needed publication, but things kept getting in the way of her writing. Summer visitors, then a trip out to Phoenix to be with her father who had broken his hip. The yard needed color. She wanted to plant impatiens and oleanders, then some vitex against erosion on the dunes. Last year there had been natural pockets of firewheel and dewberry, but the wind-flung salt from the hurricane had killed them.

If you intend to adhere to a tacky turnover policy, I'd suggest you see to it that the food leaves the kitchen in a more timely way instead of pressuring patrons to hurry up and leave . . . Julia, as she grew older, was more sensitive to noise and would say something about that too. She listened to Chad strip the bed where her sister, Norma, and Jack had slept. The washer churned loudly beyond the wall. That raccoon woman was like a black spot that wouldn't come clean. Julia's fingers assaulted the keys: *Most people go to a restaurant to forget time, relax; they don't want to be made to feel they are on a speeding conveyor belt.* Not bad. As a teacher, Julia had to submit to evaluation, why not this bratty restaurant owner?

Chad came into her study. "What's up?"

She darkened the screen. "Just writing," she said.

"That Marquez thing?"

She was relieved. "You remembered."

"How is it going?"

"Not. I've got to focus."

"You're crabby," he teased. "Must be the she crab soup last night, all that cream sauce."

"Chad, please." Perhaps he *did* know.

"You liked it then?"

"I didn't," she said.

"I'm going to mow the lawn. Chuck the sheets in the dryer when the washer stops."

By the way, I'd use mints if I were you. You've got a taint to your breath that's discernible even from a distance. And when you're huffing and rude, it's even worse. No, too strong. That, the boob tattoo, and the raccoon business were all wrong for the beginning.

The motor roared at regular intervals under the window. She tried to ignore it, then got up and opened the drapes. Chad was pushing the mower, making smaller and smaller rectangles in the grass. Lean and slightly stooped, he had a thick mustache and wore his hair long. The early morning sky was streaked with red and avenging purple. That woman needed to be stung, but first coax her in, keep her reading. *My party and I had a mixed experience at Chez Amis on Saturday evening but before getting to that, let me congratulate you. . . . The new building is beautifully appointed, tastefully done. It was the high quality of the cuisine that made us follow you to your new location.* Wait. Not high quality. Why give that brat a thing?

Neck shiny with sweat, Chad stood by the window. Two kids on jet skis snarled down the cove. Julia looked up at a long low cloud that billowed in the middle and seemed to be disemboweling itself over the band of cordgrass and scrub that grew on the dredge islands along the channel. Chad said, "Do you think we made a mistake?"

"Moving down here? I did after the hurricane."

"Maybe I shouldn't have retired."

"You didn't retire, you're tending bar, driving taxi."

"I know, but—"

"Come on, sweetheart, you got twenty years in, you never *got* shot or *had* to shoot anybody. I'd say that was lucky."

"Pero, señora, son las cosas mas malo. Worser teeng dan shooting. But I tell you, den I habe to keel you."

Julia laughed. Chad loved to throw broken Spanish at her now and then. They met when he enrolled in her conversational Spanish course at the community college, a course required for certain undercover cops and paid for by the city.

"Jack and your sister left early enough to be around Richmond by now."

"I wish they had a better time here," she said.

"Factoid. One of every four Americans is unbalanced."

"Basta, ya!"

"They had a *great* time. What's the matter with you? You can't control the weather. Hey, we went out in the boat, we went swimming, we caught some flounder. They had a good time, believe me."

But Julia wanted it to be perfect, and that fucking raccoon woman . . . It was maddening. Chad was toweling his face, saying something about a general.

"Franco. When he was close to death, his supporters were outside the palace windows yelling that."

"Yelling what?" asked Julia.

"'Adios, Generalissimo.'"

"What's the point?"

"Well, the old general supposedly popped awake and said, 'Where are they going?'"

Chad's eyes almost disappeared. He laughed more than anyone else at his own jokes. Sometimes he couldn't help himself. His way of relating to people was to tease and joke.

"Chad, jokes about somebody old and close to dying—"

"I know, I'm sorry," he said. "What do you say we play some tennis before the sun gets too high?"

"I'm not really in the mood, sweetheart."

"C'mon! Before I take a shower."

She groaned. "Give me a few minutes, I have to finish this paragraph."

She stared at the Goya and Piranesi copies that hung above her desk, then back at the laptop screen. She cut the remark about bad breath and pasted it at the bottom of the letter, for later use perhaps. Chad had made her feel as if caught red-handed. The Marquez essay wasn't getting written. What if Chad had said, *Let's have a look.* She thought of that movie with Jack Nicholson in a snowbound hotel, hugely empty, a writer who has typed, to his wife's final horror, nothing but a box full of pages with one repeated sentence: *All work and no play makes Jack a dull boy.*

They drove to the tennis courts, which were empty. It was hot and the dying cicadas pulsed like a headache at full volume. She missed easy shots at the net. Her stance was too often open, the footwork not there. And she didn't like being told so by Chad. Julia walked to a ball by the fence. She bent and smacked the ball with her racket into a flurry of bounces, perfectly controlled. There was a cawing overhead. She squinted at a fish crow being chased, it seemed, by two smaller parts of itself. Chad, too, was craning his neck. This bird kick of his. Is that a sanderling or a sandpiper, she'd ask. "Neither," he'd say, "a ruddy turnstone. They look like flying chocolate sundaes." Another time, he said, "House finches—they're just sparrows splashed with cranberry juice." Once she caught him with binoculars looking at two girls in bikinis across the cove. What was he looking at? "Pert-breasted man-catchers," he said. But nothing was funny, not today. Norma was gone, and in four days they had barely touched the subject of elder care for their father. He couldn't continue to live alone—they agreed on that—but nothing was settled. She watched the fish crow dive and swerve, now only one smaller bird in relentless pursuit.

She showered and caught herself in the mirror. Her skin color was good but perhaps a bit too dark from the sun. Her hair had lots of light, but with a thread or two of gray, brown eyes shaded by long lashes. After two children, she hadn't put on or taken off too much weight. The days of a two-piece were over though. She threw back her shoulders and flattened her belly. The way of all flesh. But Chad loved the body that was becoming less and less hers, she sometimes felt. She met her own gaze, challenging: *Jealous of her long limbs and perfect skin? Or are you some kind of martyr to taste, your body bleeding from the shafted insults of yahoos?* She leaned in close. Sunspots and freckles on her cheeks. She had been telling Chad they needed a bimini top for the skiff so they wouldn't get so much sun. She looked at herself sideways, then front. A few days ago, from the guest room down the hall, she had heard her sister's faint cry, as if in amazement, while making love, then fainter moans, the headboard tapping the wall.

Somebody with a kid's voice answered the phone. He laughed, sounded stoned. Wait staff? Dishwasher? Julia said she wanted to send some flowers to the owner, but she had forgotten her name. The kid said, "Wendy Hilliard." Then he laughed again and said it rhymed with billiard.

Julia sat at her desk, staring at the Piranesi, ropes and pulleys dangling in dim light, tiny crouched figures. She imagined this Wendy person coming into the restaurant, empty in the morning, chairs on top of tables, with a bundle of envelopes from the post office box. She would be in a good mood. The place had been full for the last two nights. Loud. People laughing and hooting, congratulating her on the new building, the great bar, various appointments, complimenting her for hiring such a fine jazz pianist. Now she would enter the kitchen, her husband at first half hidden by the hanging pans. He would be cutting vegetables and preparing sauces. The behind-the-scenes genius. He would get friendly with his hands and she would laugh, then go upstairs to the little office in the loft. She would leaf through the bills, then come to envelopes that were addressed by hand: well-wishers and friends. Then Julia's letter. Her smile would vanish, her features slacken, darken, her eyes brim, the mascara run. *The restaurant closes at*

11:00 p.m. Have you ever wondered, you shallow little puddle, why your husband doesn't get home until three in the morning? Washing dishes? Talking sports with the barman? Don't bet on it.

She stood from her chair and walked to the doorway. The feeder, a Plexiglas tube full of seed, moved slightly in the middle of the window. The pegs were empty. Chad dove off the end of the dock into water green as the Chinese tea her father loved.

Chad said, "Look, I've got to work tonight. Let's do something. It's a beautiful day. Let's take the skiff, check out the osprey chicks at that channel marker nest, then run by Chimney Island over to Beaufort for some lunch at the Verandah."

"We're being extravagant," she said, "and we just had one bad experience."

"That was dinner and it wasn't that bad."

"You didn't talk to that bitch of a hostess."

"That wasn't at the Verandah. Hey, let's do lunch." He laughed. "I've always wanted to say that."

Bogue Sound was a smooth glaze, only a cat's paw wrinkle of wind here and there on the water. They idled out of the marina past the No Wake sign. Each piling had a different bird—pelican, royal tern, laughing gull—and possession of the piling constantly changed. Chad laughed and said, "Sort of gives new meaning to time sharing."

Julia put the skiff on plane and wove her way between the red and green buoys until she came to the hotel, where she swerved and put the bow on the radio tower across the water. A deep but unmarked channel cut through the sand flats. Chad rode in front of the console on the cooler seat, loving the wind that pressed back his jet black hair. Every now and then he turned to smile at her, extend his arms and look up, as if giving thanks for the whole thing. *Many things can ruin or negate an otherwise fine meal . . .*

The sun and moving clouds turned the water over the sand flats from limpid green to indigo to black.

In the shade of the carport, Chad had the hood of his red Wrangler up, tools on the fender. In his greasy hand, the timing gun was stuttering white light. "Hey, what's up?"

"I've been thinking," she said. "I'm going to get a couple pampas grass plants for the dune on either side of the drive."

"Whoa! Pampas grass? Sweetheart, are you sure?"

"It will hold the dune, and it grows fast," she said.

"That's the trouble though. That stuff's worse than kudzu. I read about it. Remember what what's-her-name said?"

"Millie."

"Right. It *looks* nice, but it *takes over,* spreads. A home for mice and snakes. In the fall you have to burn it or chainsaw it."

A TV news program showed videotape footage from a surveillance camera of a drunk being smacked around by a cop. The bars of a holding cell were in the background, the booking counter in the foreground. The cop banged the drunk's head against the counter and knocked him unconscious. He lay unmoving on the floor, hands cuffed behind his back. The tape showed policemen joking and stepping over the body as they went about their business. The man lay there for a long time.

Chad sighed. "Man, guys like that give every cop a bad name."

Julia asked why they would do something like that.

Chad said, "Well, it's only one guy who did it."

"But the others went along."

"There could be a number of reasons. The worst is that some guys are psychos or think that kind of stuff is funny."

"Or?"

"Or there's a history here, some kind of payback."

"Payback?"

"What's this sudden curiosity?" he asked.

"I don't know, I'm just curious."

"Well, payback for getting kicked, bitten, or punched in the process of an arrest or something. Payback usually means tighten the cuffs, a few nightstick shots to the ribs. But you controlled yourself. Nothing like *this!*"

Wind and rain lashed the house. Julia was working her way through *The Pillars of Hercules.* Next summer, she and Chad wanted to see some of the great Mediterranean places. Julia had learned her Spanish in Mexico and Puerto Rico, and especially wanted to visit Spain, experience that version of the language, but the author's description made the Costa Brava seem tawdry and depressing, bullfighting unjustifiably cruel, which she knew had to be true. Reading in the evening often made her sleepy, but the story suddenly came alive and awakened her interest. The author, bound for the Syrian coast, was in a car out of gas, stranded in the desert. The wind howled. Alone, he was plagued by memories of injustice, insults, lost arguments, abusive comments, put-downs, and humiliations that went back many years. He couldn't under-stand his feelings, was at their mercy, mentally removed in a deep and frightening way from his surroundings, unable to laugh his way out, tormented, uncertain the mood would ever lift.

She heard a noise in the side yard. When Chad was gone, she was more alert to the various noises of the house, its settlings and creakings, the clack of the icemaker, the on and off hum of the air conditioner. She wondered if he took his revolver when he drove the taxi. A driver had been murdered in Jacksonville. She tried to read again, but saw the raccoon woman moving her short-skirted legs between tables. Finally her mind gave in to the book. For a while she was in a small Turkish seaport, then, sleepy, in Albertson's supermarket in Phoenix, shopping for her father. She saw a familiar woman. Mary her name was. She was one of "the breakfast club" of four or five women Julia's mother went to McDonald's with after morning Mass. Mary was tall and elegant-looking, had beautiful hands, and was a retired teacher. She had not seen this woman since the funeral. When Julia called her name, Mary's cheeks and mouth seemed to struggle with each other. Then the woman turned and hurried away down the aisle, looking once over her shoulder by the check-out. Julia was confused. The dream made it worse, kept replaying Mary's flight down the aisle.

The phone rang. She sat upright on the sofa for a moment before realizing where she was. The kitchen clock said eleven. It was Chad checking in on his cell phone. They said "Hey" to each other, imitating southerners.

"Gotcha," he said.

"What do you mean?"

"Sleeping on the job."

"Reading."

"Factoid. Did you know that Americans spend more money on cat food than books?"

"I believe it."

"Factoid. Sixteen hundred tornados a year touch down in the U.S."

"I know, weather's terrible tonight. Are you busy?"

"One fare up to Newport, two couples to the airport. Then an old woman at the Dunescape condos had me pick up a prescription for her at the pharmacy. Not much. How's the essay going?"

"So so."

It was after eleven. Normally she was in bed reading. The dream left her partly in Phoenix. She remembered her father in the living room, the television roaring. He refused to wear the new hearing aid she had gone to great lengths to have him fitted for. His right side was partially paralyzed and he didn't have the coordination to turn the volume wand. It was painful to watch him remove the tiny flesh-colored plug from his ear, struggle to raise the volume only to find it was too loud once the unit was back in his ear. Chad once asked him how the new hearing aid was working and her father replied, *Twenty minutes past five.* But this time she had flown out to Phoenix by herself. Men were pitiful without women, and the memory of her mother—palpable everywhere in the furnishing of the house—was why he refused to move. She surveyed the pictures of the Infant of Prague, the Sacred Heart, and Our Lady of Lourdes. Sitting in the chair, her father dozed with his head tilted to one side, his mouth open. Each time she woke him he said no, he was watching the news, and quickly nodded off again. She couldn't risk letting him get himself to bed. She was also afraid he might take the wrong medication. For fourteen hours he lay on the kitchen floor before being found by the visiting nurse.

In the morning, from the kitchen, she saw it and froze. Slowly, she edged toward the wall. It was small enough, judging from what Chad had said. The changing angle continued to improve the outside light. Finally she saw a spot of scarlet on the breast. She began to whisper "painted bunting" as if to make it so, but the bird was dusty brown elsewhere, like a sparrow. She groaned. It was one of those that Chad said were splashed in cranberry juice. She couldn't think of its name. It was like a tramp with a red carnation.

A bright sun made the surface of the cove a field of glitter. She squinted and tried to figure it out. Analysis, interpretation. After all that's what she did for a living. Still. She saw this Wendy person as a maggot in the brain, patiently eating away all other thoughts until only an image of herself prevailed, standing there at the table with the reservation clipboard and short skirt that showed lots of graceful leg. Her eyes were black as hornets. She slowly shook her head no. Time was up. There would be no dessert or after-dinner drinks at the table. She flipped her hair and pointed to the bar where rowdy fishermen from the Blue Water Tournament stood two and three deep. Then she stabbed her finger with a long crimson nail at Julia, repeating the turnover policy. She slitted her raccoon eyes and smiled smugly, again shaking her springy hair and flipping it back. *No, I clearly remember informing you that we have a seventy-minute turnover policy.* That penetrating, cartoon voice, those meager lips with plum lipstick. She was implying that Julia was a liar. All this in front of her sister and brother-in-law. Julia wanted to smack the smugness from her Kewpie-doll cheeks. It was unacceptable. The day was dazzling, the sky full of clouds like puffs of breath.

Chad got a phone call and within a few hours was flying up to Washington. A friend had been shot, an old partner. Instead of returning to the house from the airport where she had driven him, Julia decided to stay away from her study and drive to Wilmington, the closest city with decent malls and stores. There was a shortcut, Route 172, that Chad had taken once through Camp Lejeune. She checked her makeup in the mirror. At the north gate, a Marine left the sentry house, saluted, and asked where she was headed. Humidity and heat flooded into the car. He took his time, looking at her legs and breasts. She wondered if the shortcut through the base was worth the drooling appraisal. Finally he gave her a pass to surrender at the south gate and said something about maneuvers. She set the cruise at fifty-five miles per hour. Moody green trees flowed past. *When I suggested you might be alienating patrons, you began to lecture me about the success of your old beachfront establishment, as if I had never been there, as if you had never seen my face, as if I were some dim-witted schoolgirl and—*

A tank pulled out of the woods and stopped in the middle of the road. It pivoted its turret so that the cannon was aimed right at her windshield, the muzzle showing a wide black hole. She slammed on the breaks. Suddenly there was a soldier at her window, his face painted black and olive, branches of fresh green leaves stuck in the net of his helmet so that she seemed to be looking more at a walking bush than a man. He tapped on the window. She lowered it.

"Your pass, ma'am. Don't be alarmed. We've got war games all week. The opposition is trying to sneak a civilian vehicle through."

"What did I do?"

"Ma'am, you took a right instead of a left at that fork in the road back air."

"I'm sorry."

"Make your U-turn and proceed."

She eased forward and noticed four HumVees camouflaged at the side of the road. Soldiers had machine guns at the ready.

She sat on the back deck of Pursser's, a good lunch place she had heard about. She was reading a newspaper, drinking coffee, and watching boats. A two-masted sloop held in the current, waiting for the wings of the bridge to open. A Robalo with a maroon bimini came under the bridge and slid into one of the floating finger piers. Two couples climbed out.

The waitress asked if she would like dessert or more coffee.

"Just coffee," she said, turning the pages of her newspaper. There was an article about the president being sued for sexual harassment.

The foursome came to sit at an adjacent table under the awning. "Sawbones" was lettered on the side of their boat. Julia guessed the man with salt-and-pepper hair was a surgeon. He was tall, his leather face full of seams. They were all laughing. Gin and tonics arrived. The women got up and went down the porch toward the two doors marked Buoys and Gulls. They were younger than the men, no strap lines on their shoulders, no dimples on their thighs. One carried a red bag with Cayman Islands lettered in yellow.

Julia stirred her coffee and looked at a distant catamaran with blue and white sails.

"This place we ate at," said the doctor, "was run by these two lesbos."

His friend laughed.

"They *was*. Real butch. Good food though."

"You ever eat at the Red Onion?"

"I can't say we have."

"Stan, the chef, used to be at the Plantation. Remember him?"

"I'll never forget his crusted triggerfish with herbs," said one of the women as she sat down.

The doctor said, "We was just talking about Stan. Isn't he a fabulous chef, Shug?"

She said he was.

"Well, anyway, he's at this new place."

"Good, this coast can always use another good restaurant. Eating is what we like to do when we come down here."

"Don't forget drinking," howled the woman with the Caymans bag, unwrapping her silverware from the napkin.

They all hooted. "We do plenty of that."

"Have you ever tried Café 58?"

The doctor's face stiffened. "I don't go there no more. The hostess, this little college twit, she gave our reservations to these two old geezers." He turned to his wife. "We was only five or ten minutes late, wuddn't we, Shug?"

"That's right."

"Well, sir, I tore that little gal's head off, ripped it right off. True. I heard she quit that very night. They say she puked in the loo. Owner had to hostess himself for a few weeks and"—limping his wrist—"he didn't even have an evening dress. She wouldn't come back to work, no how, no way. Good is what I say. We drove fifteen miles from the other end of the island to see these geezers in walkers take our table. She goes, 'I'm sorry, sir, but our policy'— Like we was nobody. Well, not this piggy."

Chad drove the only time they were in Wilmington. Now she was lost. After the mall, she had taken a wrong turn and kept on going until she was in a beach town and saw the aquarium sign. A friend had told her about the aquarium. She parked and went into the dim light. It was nice and cool. The exhibits glowed behind glass and various kinds of fish drifted back and forth. One tank had reef fish, bright as jewels, but she was mesmerized by the skates and rays coming out of the gloom and into focus. The skates undulated their outer edges, advanced, and hovered. The bat rays flew like hawks, slowly beating their great wings. Sharks in the bigger tank slid by making circles and figure eights, lacing back and forth in slow motion. The eerie eyes of a shark seemed to catch hers each time it went past in its unhappy prison.

When Chad phoned from D.C., she asked how his friend Eddie was doing. Eddie had a round baby face and was always trying to control his weight, the target of lots of food humor from the guys.

Chad said it had been a routine pull-over and the driver shot him, a drug dealer. A long list of priors. The doctor was being cautious, but Eddie might easily be in a wheelchair for the duration.

"Remember you asked me about payback that night?"

She said yes.

"Well, I hadn't thought of this in a long time. Remember I used to ride with Crazy Elmo?"

Julia had only met Elmo once, but he had unforgettable hard black eyes and the most chilling look she had ever seen, totally gung ho. Even other cops were afraid of him.

"I remember."

"Well, there was this black guy he arrested, and the guy walked on a technicality, made faces at Elmo when he left the court room, *not* the kind of thing anybody who isn't really crazy would do to Elmo. These guys are all repeaters, right? So one night seven or eight months later, Elmo busts the guy again, but this time the guy pulls a knife before the cuffs go on. Imagine! But Elmo doesn't do anything, even verbally taunt the guy the way he usually does. He whistles the Disney tune, you know, *Hi ho, hi ho, it's off to work we go.* But you can tell something's going on. So midway downtown, he draws his gun and puts it to the guy's head, tells the guy to jump out of the car or he'll kill him. At this point the guy must have realized Elmo was crazier than he was. So he jumps. You could see in the rearview the guy bouncing around like a rag doll. Cars sideswiping each other to avoid running him over. Elmo then turns around, calls the rescue squad, and adds 'attempting to escape' to the list of charges. Guy's in a wheelchair to this day. True story."

"I'm not sure I wanted to hear that."

Chad's plane wasn't getting in until seven something. She remembered the shark and Dr. Sawbones. She knew she had to get out of the house. After some coffee, she drove to the nursery. A different kind of concentration was required—she somehow knew that. Today her thoughts seemed willing to stay with the questions of portulaca or lantana, the problems of arrangement in the yard. The nursery offered lots of other color, but she finally settled on oleanders, three white and three red. In Phoenix, oleander seemed to thrive in the heat. There was a wall of them fifteen feet high that divided her father's yard from the neighbors. Lots of white bloom. On the coast, they never got more than four or five feet high, but they would stay bright during the summer months. The nursery woman recommended, especially for the coastal sand, a rich potting soil, peat moss, and mulch. If Julia worked quickly, there was no reason she couldn't have the oleander in and flanking the driveway before Chad returned. And she did. She had shoveled, hauled on her hands and knees, rounded the holes, measured the depth, and set in the plants. With pine straw on top, the plants would stay moist. A neat job, except for the pine needles that would have to be vacuumed from the back of Chad's pride-and-joy red Wrangler.

That smug little Kewpie-doll face . . . smeared lipstick and mascara . . . you look like a clown . . . a circus performer shot from the cannon one too many times. Rereading what she had written made her shudder. Bat rays and sharks came at her out of the gloom. She thought for a moment and somehow became aware of her hands. She held them up and turned them in the light, then told her fingers to highlight the whole letter. She smiled, then stabbed the delete key. The screen went white.

She went into the living room and slumped into the big armchair facing the bay window on the cove. She thought about Chad and his friend Eddie in the hospital. It was noon in Phoenix. She hoped the woman from Friendly House found her father awake and alert. She would phone in a while to see how he was doing. First she would put on her bathing suit and dive off the dock. She felt good. Something had been accomplished. When they pulled in the drive, he would see the oleanders. The sun was getting low. She became aware of a bird on the feeder. It was the size of a sparrow but looked more slender. She eased to the floor below the sofa and crawled on her belly out of the bird's line of sight, to retrieve the binoculars. It was what Chad had wanted her to see. "Painted bunting," she said softly. He was magnificent, scarlet underparts, metallic blue head, greenish wings, a patch of bright yellow on his back. He poked his beak into the feeder and chewed quickly. She watched him for a long time. Finally other birds darted in and bumped him from the feeder. Black, gray, red, blue, they replaced each other with the suddenness of thought and mood.

True Colors

Dana watches Lee for a minute, then dunks her brush in the bucket of suds. At the end of the next finger pier, even if he can't quite see her or his own boat, mostly hidden by the bow of a Bayliner, Lee, if he listened, could hear Dana's steady brush getting blood from the deck, or her hose scooting suds through the scuppers. This kind of quiet is deep enough for someone to drown in, she thinks, the kind Lee would rather fill with talk amplified by beer. Instead, as if to devil him, from a schooner, anchored just outside the cove, its portholes already yellow, drifts an Italian aria. Lavender light and reflection make the schooner unreal, partly her own creation.

Another Sunday afternoon. Almost nine months' worth. She buckets the long-handled brush, then appraises the lingering blue light on the docks. To the west, the light above the tree line, coming down on the still waters of Bogue Sound, is misty gold. Mosquitoes are starting to whine. Without them, you could forget who you are, where you are, and just slide back to childhood on vivid color. Lee, though, is oblivious, needs to hurry, finish cleaning his prize, a thirty-pound bull dolphin.

The bow of the Bayliner dips after a swell, leaving him visible for a moment at the cleaning table, above which there is a light, not yet on. Dana gets a glimpse of those well-muscled legs and arms, long hair, blond and curly. Banana Republic safari shorts. Dana wonders, would mosquitoes make him gesture like that? Unlikely. Lee was always performing, like the night she met him, amusing everyone with impersonations of movie stars and stories about cut-up times in high school, the unbelievable things he'd done, places he'd been. Why not rehearse and perform for himself, an audience of one? Now, a cutout figure made dramatic by low light and isolation at the end of the dock, he seems on stage as he looks off into the distance, points seaward, then tables his beer, bending to work his knife against the whetstone. His father taught him how to fillet. Sharp knife does it all, his father used to say, and Lee loves to quote that line to anyone who puts him into the spotlight while he is steaking a wahoo or filleting a grouper. But it's Sunday, late, Labor Day gone, no summer people, especially women—no spotlight. Almost like being skunked. Only a few owners move between boats, making sure of the mooring lines one last time, getting the cat's cradle just right, so the boat can't touch either piling or dock.

Even at this distance, she can see his lips move. What invisible person stands at his side out there? Caught in the act, he'll redden. OK, so he talks to himself—he admits it, but would you rather be caught talking to yourself, or picking your nose? Devil makes him do it, and the devil makes him pay. No laugh, a pitchfork right in the neck. He shrugs, rotates his head—the old football neck getting stiff again, worse now, he tells people, for tackling that guy in a ski mask he caught running from a Zip Mart with a fist full of money. On the way to the condo, he'll pop a couple Advil and wash them down with another Corona from the cooler. But the show must go on. You want to know the best way to make mahi-mahi out of this bull dolphin? Well, it's like this. They're really too thin to steak, and the spine has knuckles too big to make your usual slab. First rip that pretty skin off with pliers, then little by little make the fillet from dorsal to belly instead of head to tail. Oh, he got this one southwest of Big Ten Fathom, six miles past the trawler wreck, just out of sight of land. Good fight. Forty minutes on light tackle.

The old gentleman asking the questions knows the location, but he has never been there himself. Flounder drifting is *his* favorite kind of fishing. Peaceful. He doesn't need the drama of the big fight, fish that leap and tail-walk on the line. Flounder drifting is quiet, you kill the motor. Lee looks up from the thin line of blood his incision has made from belly to dorsal on the silver skin. This dignified old gent has pale blue eyes, hollow cheeks, and fine white hair like the spun glass on a seawitch lure. Heavy accent. Lee is better at catching fish than catching names. Was it Dudley?

When he looks down again, blood has smeared and ruined the iridescent blue and yellow gold of the dolphin's dorsal and flank, but that will now come off with the pliers, a ripping sound like pulled adhesive tape. He's working faster, against the failing light, Mr. Dudley telling him to be careful. After all, there's all kinds of time. Impatience is the mark of an amateur. Lee doesn't want a scar like this, does he? Mr. Dudley holds his palm to the light. Champeen scar. He has cleaned lots of fish in his time. No more. Son does that. But he's in college, just left for his senior year.

From the schooner, a second voice, a tenor, joins the first.

Small things, says Mr. Dudley, small things are what make him happy now. Just being able to micturate. Now there was a word for you: micturate. He learned it in the hospital. Did you ever realize how good it felt just to be able to take a good old race-horse piss? He'd been all plugged up. Cysts. But Mr. Dudley has a great doctor. He's only been out of the hospital for a week. And the blood's finally gone from his urine. Ah, that feels good. Lord, the things we take for granted.

Next thing I knew, Lee might later say, I heard the sound of splattering water. What a character this Mr. Dudley was, Lee might say, going on about nature and beauty and what we take for granted. Well, he was a beauty for sure, and the moral is never take anything for granite, unless it's a gravestone.

No laugh though. The old gentleman is pale, looks lonely, and might have lost his wife. Lee knows about loss. He has told colleagues he was orphaned at nine, parents killed in a car wreck. Traumatized, he never learned to read until he was sixteen. But Dana has met his parents, his mother going on in front of Lee's "new girl" about how precocious Lee was, a fluent preschool reader, verbally gifted. Another time, at a cocktail party, he encouraged his internist, Dr. Glover, to lament having to put his dear ol' mama into a rest home. Listening thoughtfully, as he always does, Lee nodded, then said how it put him in mind of his own parents, also in a rest home. Yes, he knew about these painful decisions. In confidential tones, he said his mother too was a two-pack-a-day smoker and an alcoholic who almost burned the family house down, and that was before she came down with Alzheimer's. Dr. Glover seemed heartened, his eyes moist and bright.

These confidences make Lee feel good, close to others, but he knows, has to know what some people say, has to have heard the joke about himself: *The fairy tale begins, Once upon a time; the Lee tale begins, That reminds me of the time . . .* Stung, he thinks no doubt about his first wife, Dawn, who was a psycho about truth, he says. If you think about it, he says, tampering a little bit with the factual can be charitable, even healing, if not liberating. Anyway, what I'm telling you is no exaggeration, it actually happened this way! Ask Dana.

The soprano's voice becomes plaintive.

Dana watches him take a sip of his Corona, the bottle slippery with fish slime, and look out toward the schooner, that god-awful music. A few more strokes of the knife and the second fillet is off, rinsed, cut in sections, slipped into the freezer-size Ziploc. Lee holds up for admiration the three-foot skeleton, blunt head and deep V tail still intact, last light making the carcass seem like an X-ray. No waste. Before tossing it to the crabs, he punctures the eyes with the tip of his knife. Mr. Dudley winces. Otherwise, Lee explains, carcass will eventually float, stink up the docks. And that sign over the table asks you to do it. Sure, it's spooky—Out out vile jelly, and all that. If truth were told, Lee is afraid of the dark. But somehow the old man is a shield against it, the way a living parent stands between you and the dark waters.

The carcass hits the water with a loud slap, like a sound that awakens the person put to sleep by a hypnotist. Dana puts the empty bucket and brush into the cuddy cabin, still thinking about Lee and his silent gestures. She watches him wipe his sweaty face on the sleeve of the T-shirt that says "Sloppy Joe's," the only proof he was ever actually in Key West after the time he blew up. In front of friends, she gave a more sober version of something that happened to them. Then he slammed out the door and was gone for a week. Mr. Dudley notices that the shirt is the same color as water in the Keys, same pale green, pretty as daggone hell. But Florida, for Mr. Dudley, isn't a serious state, is a Republican dream. The North Carolina coast better by far. Enfield is where he's from.

Lee's lived all over the place. Of course he knows where Enfield is. That's Connecticut, right?

Not with this accent, says Mr. Dudley. They both laugh. Lee admits he is just kidding. Mr. Dudley reckons he's known a kidder or two. But what was it like out there?

Nasty. Plain nasty. Lee got thrown against the corner of the cuddy cabin door, a rib or two likely broken. He can barely breathe. The inlet was like a devil's cauldron if you want to know the truth. To catch fish, though, you've got to tough it out.

But that was odd—Mr. Dudley saw no whitecaps from his ocean-front house.

This may have been so, but Lee says you don't need whitecaps in order to have steep seas. The words repeat themselves: steep seas. Mr. Dudley's weathered face and fine-spun white hair press into the corners of Lee's vision. Steep seas. Some things and some people just rattle you, nickel-and-dime you to death. About certain things, Dawn was pathological, absolutely. Dana knows the mere mention of her name can lock him into a snit. No whitecaps, my ass. Lee hoses small bloody pieces of meat and skin through the hole at the back of the unpainted plywood table. The quiet is heavy, awful. Mosquitoes keen. The last drops of water plink. Amber lights come on all along the marina walkways. In the gazebo too out on one of the jaws of the cove. Just beyond the gazebo, the schooner barely moves on its white reflection. Mr. Dudley is gone. Not even an I-enjoyed-talking-to-you. The tenor's voice echoes the sad phrases of the soprano. Dana hums along.

The dock vibrates with Lee's heavy footfalls, closer and closer. She can hear him behind a big Sea Ray, but he whistles as if to announce himself. He tells her she did a great job on the teak. And Rainex worked real good on the windshield. He holds up the freezer bag full of meat and chants "Di-di-di-daah!"

"Beethoven can be catchy," she says.

"Don't believe it," he says.

She knows that, once home, fish in the freezer, he'll want to make love. "Why did you take a leak off the end of the dock?"

"I didn't," he says.

"It must have been somebody else I saw."

"I was talking to this little kid," he says, "Maybe he took a squirt while I wasn't looking."

"You sure it wasn't an old man?"

"Maybe your daddy's come to visit," he says. "After all, he's up and traveling now."

Maybe I was imagining something about your mother, she almost says, but the ground then would be uncertain as quicksand.

Instead, she smiles and asks him where he caught that big manly fish.

"Oh, out yonder," he says.

"Was it stormy out there?"

He squints. "You crazy, Lady Bug? It was a millpond. You was there, dontcha remember?"

In only months, she has learned his lingo, his routines, his games, but as soon as she knows a game well enough to improvise, he changes the rules. He's either less than meets the eye, or more, much more.

"You're losing it," he says. "You're always ready, *like somebody else I know,* to make something outta practically nothing. Here's tomorrow night's meal."

Hopping up from the cockpit to the dock, she hefts the freezer bags, then buries them in the rattling ice of the cooler. Takes a deep breath. The schooner mirrors itself on pastel water. She could just stand here and listen to that music, but soon it would end. Endings are tricky, often a mess. She would have to be careful. I'm not losing a thing, she thinks. Suddenly she laughs and, grabbing one handle of the big cooler, says, "C'mon, Hoss, let's saddle up, get these cattle to Abilene."

Existential Dirty Jokes

Lynda had left him. The house grew haunted. The days, for Colin, slurred past, but night after night an accusing beam from the lighthouse made the bedroom leap out of its shadows. "You don't want a wife," she had said, "You want a fucking maid!" That was months ago, but he still winced, for it was soap opera, worse. Almost everybody now said "fucking." No longer was it just for sailors and construction workers; it had made the Big Time, was blessed by appearance in the *New Yorker* and, Colin thought, might sooner or later make its way into church liturgy.

Lynda was a great scene-maker. In front of his friend Kirby, she said, "I'll tell you what,"—she walked around slamming drawers and assembling her things—"you better just hire a housekeeper." Her blonde hair sprang like a slinky. "What in hell do you know about *me?*" But before he could reply, she said, "Existentialism, the fucking absurd—don't make me laugh!" She snorted. *"You're* absurd! *Diddley* is what you fucking know!"

No matter, he knew he would be empty, full of hurt when she left. Reason and Emotion—they weren't even strange bedfellows. He also knew clichés, exposed them in student papers, grabbed them by the scruff, and gave them the bum's rush.

Like a student, he had been tested and found wanting. First by

Betty, now Lynda, who hated his openness, his brooding inquiry, and might have stayed if only he had a better sense of humor, surprised her with something out of character: *You can't shit on a man with a turd in his pocket.* Something like that, some folk aphorism Kirby might coin. But that wasn't Colin's style; in fact, he didn't know if he had a style. Others did.

So her new Mustang burned rubber the length of Sea Winds Way, the radio blaring an old Nancy Sinatra tune. She might have been headed toward some Texas Lonestar of the mind.

Kirby stood in the middle of the half-painted kitchen. Luckily on hand after Lynda's soapy exit, Kirby provided solace, so Colin had to feel a certain gratitude, but Kirby was a great dispenser of advice, and perhaps enjoyed the role too much, pried in a friendly way, asked impertinent questions about their sex life. Rocking on his heels, eyes blue as seawater, he sipped coffee dramatically, as if such were a prerequisite to serious thought, of which he was incapable for prolonged periods. His sunburned nose, like a strawberry, presided over a face deeply tanned, eyes whitely crinkled. He had recently bought a twenty-six-foot Grady with a few seasons on it, fully rigged for deep sea, and offered stories of big tuna and wahoo boated or lost after epic struggles, stories of stormy seas and danger skillfully evaded—all for Colin's approval and admiration, admitting Colin was very different, Colin had mental depths beyond reckoning, but his flaky style could easily have been the problem.

"You ought to get out," Kirby suggested.

"Out?"

"Right, o-u-t. That funny smell outside—it's fresh air."

"As a matter of fact, I'm just now going to Robyn's."

"Ah yes"—as W. C. Fields—"a sweet thing, but potentially—"

"Kirby, please."

"All I'm saying is you're vulnerable. Think of the boxing ring— Protect yourself at all times."

Colin held up his hand: stop.

But Kirby went on: "You're a garden of wonderful thoughts, but you don't know people, what they need."

"Exactly what Lynda used to say. Did you go to bed with her?"

"Please—we were *friends*." Kirby pointed to the dead screen of the TV: "You see the news last night?"

"I did."

"Well?"

"Having a wild bear loose in the neighborhood is at least interesting."

"Not that, the Len Bias thing," said Kirby.

"Oh that."

"Oh that," he mimicked. "See, what matters to most people doesn't touch you. Hey, I'm no fucking philosopher, but I know what I know."

"What do you know?"

"I know you've got to get your shit together. Think about particulars for a while."

"What particulars?"

"Look at this rat's nest, this kitchen that *Lynda* began painting and you'll never finish. Never mind your car always running out of gas or, ah, the lost book that turns up in your freezer."

While Kirby outlined the things that Colin needed to deal with, Colin could hear him with grad students at the Library Bar: . . . *really bright guy, but doesn't know to come out of the rain, his old Lincoln with the opera window always running on Empty. Sometimes, though, it works in his favor. Some kids hotwired his car one night and ran out of gas before they turned the corner. Another time . . .*

"Hear me?" He coughed and deepened his voice. "Earth to Colin, come in, please."

Colin stood in the kitchen, trying to follow a recipe. He diced carrots and de-veined shrimp. *Semper paratus*—from years ago in the Boy Scouts, the motto so important. But he wasn't prepared when Lynda left. Nor Betty before. He had forgotten how to do for himself. Rarely had he done laundry, never had he cooked. Compared to his intellectual pursuits, these things seemed profoundly unimportant. Nikolai Berdyaev had marveled at a friend's ability to change a lightbulb. Colin knew he wasn't that bad. But after Lynda's harsh accusations, he kept coming back to a scene on the fourth floor of Sugg Hall, just a week before finals. Sugg's shadowy reaches and stairwells seemed designed by Piranesi, a great place for the unspeakable, and without elevators, the Rescue Squad took a lifetime to arrive. Jackson lay on the floor, skin bluish. Colin hated himself and the others who stood around not knowing what to do, men who knew everything about Hegel and Flaubert, but nothing about how to help poor Jackson who, prone on the chocolate tiles, eyes bugging, was making mouths like an expiring flounder. They didn't even loosen his tie. Christ.

As though to accompany his mood, it began to rain. While wondering why he was holding a flashlight in the middle of the day, he remembered having intended to call Robyn. The kettle on the stove, when he looked at it, exhaled steam. He moved to turn off the burner but it was already off. He forgot, while thinking of Jackson and all the things that needed attention, that he had already made himself coffee; a warm mouthful was still left in the cup.

Diddley is what you fucking know!

He now knew how to make a Chinese meal, and finished thin-slicing the vegetables. When he had made this meal several more times and was sure of it, he would casually invite Robyn to dinner.

———

The old pink Lincoln with its rear opera windows was horribly hot; needing a tune-up Colin couldn't afford, it chugged along Front Street. He squinted into the great wallow and glitter of the sea. Jet skiers were mindlessly shooting back and forth in the baking sun.

Unaccustomed to using the teller machine, Colin was relieved to find it out of order, but the little branch bank, comatose with Muzak, seemed air-conditioned to the temperature of a walk-in freezer. Lynda had finally closed the account: it was odd to see his name all by itself on checks again, made him feel colder. A guy with something of the large-mouth bass about his face stood next to Colin at the table in the center of the room and blew a deep whistling breath through his nose. He was too big for his clothes and his hair was greasy. "You hear about it?"

Colin's eyes left the checkbook.

The man dropped his deposit slip. Holding on to the table, he stooped, cartilage crackling and popping like bacon on the fry, and grunted himself loudly to an upright position. "You will," he said, breathing with great effort from the recent strain on his hydraulic system. Colin recalled the Red Cross instructor saying that for obese victims, CPR was slightly different.

"It was on the news this morning," he said, and began to cough.

Colin saw Jackson on his back, his chest barely lifting.

The heavy man was wheezing. "Sooner or later you gone see it on the TV, so I might as well tell you." He waited.

Colin said, "I think I can take it."

"Len Bias is dead."

Colin went back to filling out his withdrawal slip.

The wheezer said, "You a basketball fan, ain'tcha?"

"Yes," Colin lied.

One of the tellers was saying that, yes, her neighborhood was where it was spotted. A customer in the next line asked, "Where what was spotted?"

"That big bear."

"The forest fire down east must have drove it this way," said another.

The wheezer shook his head. "Just when he had the world by the short hairs."

"My sister—she gone got her a satellite dish."

Colin left the table and got into line. At the drive-through window a moon-faced little girl leaned out of the car window and said her name was Emma Sue Korbett. Her voice, amplified by the speaker, filled the bank. Everyone listened. "Would you like a lollypop?" asked the teller.

There was no immediate reply. Everyone waited. Then: "I wont a hotdawg!"

Behind Colin, the wheezer gasped. Colin turned in alarm. The whisper was sadly loud: "One of the All Time Fuckin' Greats."

A graduate student in Communications, Robyn lived in an apartment over a garage behind one of the old mansions a few blocks from the waterfront. After Jackson's needless death, Colin met her in a free evening course on CPR given by the Red Cross. Only ten people: a few profs, a few students, some townspeople. She had a wonderful wink. Somehow they ended up together, and practiced ventilations and compressions on the same computerized dummy. The instructor, a hefty man who told them he was proud of his clean sense of humor, said they should all take the follow-up course: The After-effects of Mouth to Mouth or, How to Avoid Becoming Emotionally Involved with an Attractive Victim.

But it was no joke. Colin invited Robyn for a drink after the first class and their kisses became "ventilations." Colin had to restrain himself. He knew that Robyn was as drawn to him—he had to take it slow. He wanted to make love to her immediately and the desire would not go away; if anything, days made it grow more intense.

She wore goofy clothes, strap shoes and white cotton socks, gaudy print dresses—Salvation Army specials. Butterfly glasses. But underneath the willful disguise was a body with delightful proportions, the face of a Donatello angel. Robyn gave "ventilations" as if life really depended on them, but laughter was never completely out of her voice. She was bright and, for a graduate student, well read. She loved to say that everything from a certain angle was funny, and everything on TV should be viewed as entertainment. Everything. And she mocked his loves: existentialism was funny because the word had died. Hadn't he heard of the health club that called itself the Existential Body Shop? And how the Existential Vacuum now came with handy attachments? Sartre, Chestov, Berdyaev, and Camus were funny because they had no sense of humor. Berdyaev—now there's a comic genius for you! Not a single laugh in any of those guys. Kierkegaard? Didn't every kid's bicycle have one? Wasn't that Danish for chain guard? And she loved to deliver clichés: "Put yourself in my shoes." "Nothing's sacred." "That's life." "To make a long story short . . ."

Robyn's TV was always on, the VCR ready to tape whatever she might use to illustrate some research in progress. Colin stirred his coffee and listened to the rapid-fire tock tock of Robyn at her PC. The phone rang. It was Kirby.

"He wants to know if you'd like to go fishing."

Colin shook his head.

Robyn held out the phone, pressing the mute button. "Make your own excuses," she chanted. Colin took the phone, and begged off politely. When he hung up, she said, "Why not *go?*"

Colin almost said, "Why don't *you* go?" Instead: "I might get seasick."

"Try again."

"I'd be at his mercy out there."

"He just wants to show off his new boat."

"The need for flattery is a weakness, a bad habit. Besides, he didn't *make* the boat, he simply makes a lot of money moon-lighting."

Robyn seemed deliberately to ignore him. She finally said, "I think it would be a fun thing to do."

"I'm not outdoorsy. Some people just aren't. And I'm not going to be told by TV ads that I ought to feel bad about myself if I'm not out there windsurfing or something. Kirby's . . ."

"Kirby's what?"

"Put it this way—I don't try to change people."

"And Kirby does."

"Yes, and so did my ex."

She sat in his lap. "Honey, ah lubs ya like you is. Give us a great big wet ventilation. Mmmmmm!"

Back at her keyboard, she said, "I do know that Kirby, though, is a good teacher. His course was exciting, enter*tain*ing."

"Amen."

Colin stared at one of Robyn's reproductions: a Flemish burgher's wife, in slanting light, was peeling potatoes in the seventeenth century.

Someone on a soap opera said, "I just can't take it anymore."

While Robyn tocked away at her keyboard, Colin scanned the local paper: "The large black bear which led a several-hour chase of public protection officers Monday was sighted at sunset yesterday eating from a grapevine in the yard of Stanley Riggs in the Newhouse subdivision." That wasn't far away. Interested, he continued to read but the report ended abruptly with several sentences that belonged in another story—something about Hong Kong labor and counterfeit golf balls.

"Come in here," yelled Robyn, "You've got to see this." She was doing a study of commercials—a late paper for a course she was taking. "It's, ah, very existential." She hit the play button on the

VCR and a famous "presenter" held up a little box of laxative and began to hyperbolize. She cackled. "My God, you'd think the stuff was for blocked-up elephants!" By the time her tape went through several more commercials with wild claims about toothpaste and antacid formulas, she was in tears. The actor in the last had bulging hyperthyroid eyes and Robyn hit the freeze button that held the close-up face tortured by indigestion. The protruding eyes bothered Colin—he was on the fourth floor again. Jackson passed him in the hall with a smile, but looking a little pale. Colin turned and watched Jack make his way toward Sugg 451 where, at two o'clock on Tuesdays and Thursdays, he lectured on tragedy. Jackson seemed a little groggy in the legs. As Colin watched, he bumped into the wall and lurched in the other direction, staggering, a classic drunk walk until the books spilled. His hands searched the wall as if looking for a handle. Colin stood there and yelled. Jackson's eyes bulged and his face slowly got the color of eggplant.

In the heat and white sun, Colin felt confused and out of breath.

Robyn came out to the porch and yelled: "Shane, come back, Shane!"

At the light on Magnolia Street, something chanced to catch his eye. The guy stopped running. Did he wobble? It looked like Lynda's brother, Todd. The shade and sun alternated, like strobes. Colin couldn't get a good look. Pale, skinny legs, yellow jersey. What the hell was the matter with him running in this heat? Colin tried to follow, but traffic wouldn't allow a left turn. Then the motor stalled. Cars beeped and passed him. Colin turned the key and tried to think: *Determine breathing, call for help, clear the airways, then* . . . Then what? Was it two or four ventilations? Christ. Jackson lurched, his books spilling, and clawed at the wall. Todd, small in the distance, leaned against the telephone pole. The motor started and Colin swung east. Todd was making his unsteady way toward Partyfare. God, he almost fell.

Colin jumped the curb and stopped on the sidewalk so that the figure, now blacked out by the sun behind it, staggered toward his open window. Colin shaded his eyes and noticed that the person was not Todd. Swaying, the kid's smile came slowly, starting at the corners of his mouth and creeping all over his face, wrinkling the cheeks. The kid's mustache had less than twenty hairs.

"Are you all right?" Colin asked. "I was afraid . . ."

The kid closed his eyes and giggled. "You're, ah, Professor . . ." His voice was a yell until he unplugged the black sponges from his ears: a buzz of sound. He swayed, took a step, and muttered, "Fucking amazing."

Traffic delayed Colin's escape. Finally, when he succeeded in turning, the kid had already emerged from Partyfare with a six-pack and was wobbling up the street toward the TKE house.

The sky was high and vast as a cathedral, the sun a yellow circle right in the middle, mocking. A Mozart harp concerto on the FM, he found himself rolling through the countryside past tobacco barns to put himself into a better mood, but turned back to town after passing a number of ramshackle churches with signboards saying "Jesus Is Coming," "The Devil Wants Your Soul," or "God Still Speaks To Those That Take The Time To Listen." Again he thought of Robyn and, against all odds, began to smile; it was crazy. Robyn improved her mood on Sunday nights with a little preacher watching. She and her friends would have a few beers or light a joint and watch the TV preachers in their polyester suits get manic about the End Time, Sodom and Gomorrah, and hidden satanic messages on rock albums. Derlacker, another Communications major, would make a mask of toilet paper, moisten the paper, and hang it over the haranguing face of Jimmy Swaggart, cousin of the famous Jerry Lee Lewis, a "pore lost soul" who fell into the clutches of Satan and invented that scourge of scourges—rock music. "Well," said the masked man to a living room full of stoned giggles, "you cain't even call it music."

A haunted house or the Library Bar? Choice seemed limited. And Colin wasn't one of the boys, preferred the company of women, but Robyn was a temptation to be resisted, not completely, just enough to appear in control, just enough not to appear the fool, and after all, no one was such a fool or failure he couldn't kill time in a bar. Lynda was probably sitting at a bar this very moment, feeding her forgetfulness with a Lone Star, dreaming of John Travolta and the mechanical bull. Why Lynda? Why Betty? Best not dwell on it.

Kirby, Rezo, and a few grad students were watching "People's Court." Robyn would be watching the same folksy justice, cases of real people, a show that was hyped as "absolutely, undeniably real." The case involved a dogfight suit. Rezo, a no-neck guy who played in two softball leagues, barked and made snarling noises. Kirby made the usual joke about putting Colin's beer in a disposable paper cup. "Yeah," barked Rezo, "then burn the fuckin' thing when he's done with it!"

"Turn down the volume," said Jerry from behind the bar, "Christ, that fucking voice of yours could cut metal." Tall, pocked cheeks, large eyes, Jerry was a former political science prof who, for political reasons, never got tenure. He leased the bar, greased a few politicos, and weekends booked name bands into a packed barn of a back room. Horribly despondent when denied tenure, he was now, as Kirby loved to say, laughing all the way to the bank—and in a new Mercedes. Shoving a Dos Equis in front of Colin, Jerry said, "This is the best philosophy there is."

To which Colin could only think to reply: "Kirby tell you to say that?"

"Kirby? You kidding me? His jock's too tight—cuts off circulation to his brain."

Rezo hooted and, during a commercial, his gravel voice from the end of the bar joked about Christa McAuliffe and teacher burnout. Everyone laughed—Rezo and the grad students he cultivated. Two of them touched glasses and said "Throttle up."

Jerry's eyeballs rolled. He shook his head and emptied his lungs of smoke that curled slowly upward past the fluorescent tubes and lost itself against the dark ceiling. "So, whattya know?"

Colin knew that comedy could be many-sided. He saw the TKE brother deaf to the world in headphones, swaying, stoned. Was that funny? Distance made for laughter. Some things were too close. On the screen, three talking toilets slid together in a pow-wow meant to suggest women chatting. The lids moved up and down to simulate mouths in conversation. "How do you keep your bowl so clean and white?" one asked. Robyn would be laughing with eyes tightly shut. Colin noticed something dripping from the lower left corner of the TV. Maybe he imagined it. No, something was dripping.

"I know," said Jerry. "The AC. I got a guy coming in."

A TV report on the death of Len Bias took dominion. Rezo was quiet for once. A cocaine habit loomed as a faint possibility. Bias had signed with the Celtics for a huge salary. Coach and friends were interviewed: it was a tragedy. Teammates had faces shiny with tears. A reporter concluded with "To An Athlete Dying Young," while footage showed Bias taking the alley-oop, making a steal, or soaring in slow motion toward and above the rim with a ball the size of an orange in his great black hand. Water continued to leak down the side of the TV and drip on the duckboards behind the bar.

Jerry said, "Shock, sadness, business as usual. Hey, I'll tell you something—news stinks faster than those fish that Kirby gives me. I'm serious. Next week they'll be Len Bias jokes."

"Epigrams on the death of a feeling, according to Nietzsche."

But Jerry was focused on the TV. "So, ah, Jackson bit the dust?"

"I'm afraid so."

"He wasn't even fifty, was he?"

"Forty-three."

"Didn't he have tenure?"

Colin said yes, a few years ago.

"I always said tenure and death go hand in hand."

"Funny but not true," said Colin, knowing it was neither.

The bar suddenly seemed airless, like the bottom of a giant aquarium. Colin said he had to go. On the way out he stopped for a leak. On the wall above the urinal someone had written: *Life, alas, is like a penis—the harder the better.*

It looked like Rezo's scrawl.

Next to the kitchen sink, on the beige formica, a line of ants was emerging from a tiny crack near the wall. Summer again. One by one he squashed them with his forefinger and dropped them into the waste bucket beneath the sink. It could go on all afternoon. Was it wise to maximize the differences between ourselves and other forms of animal life? Colin became conscious of his hands, how they could almost live a life of their own. He had to do something, something practical. He decided to attack the skipping problem in the Lincoln, anything to keep from thinking of Lynda, to keep from running to Robyn. Plugs might do the trick. Mopping his face and neck with a handkerchief, he climbed into the Lincoln and headed for Western Auto.

One could never tell whose car might be at Robyn's place, but Colin, pulling up the long dark drive, was surprised. The apartment lights glowed softly, but he stopped just outside of their reach. He didn't know what to do and sat for some moments before backing down the drive. Parked in the cavern underneath was Kirby's red Camaro.

The lighthouse, like a toothache, pulsed throughout the long night.

Picking up his mail at the departmental office, Colin came upon Rezo in front of the bank of pigeonholes. He was talking to a grad student who had been around the department almost as long as Colin: six years.

"Dennis Johnson?"

"No," said Rezo, trying to whisper, "Think about it again. Who's the only Celtic under six feet?"

"Oh, Christ! You're twisted, man."

A flotilla of boats with brightly colored sails in the turning basin was going to force the bridge to open before he could get to it, so Colin turned into the Dockside parking lot to wait out the traffic. Seagulls seemed nailed to the pilings along the wharf. The air was full of sunset, streaked with red and purple. Five or six dolphins rolled slowly westward along the waterway, showing their fins, blowing audibly. Breath after breath. In intelligence they were supposed to be closest to humans. But gentle and wise. Aquatic philosophers from the lost Atlantis. Colin thought of a colleague and how he went for all this pseudo philosophic stuff, the hope of a transhuman level of consciousness and the rest of it. Nature, from *nasci,* to be born. Who was it, though, who said that Nature only excites expectations it can never satisfy?

Colin watched the light turn, saw color come to the tops of clouds: rose, gold, lilac. The dolphins, now backlit, sprouted momentary silver shrubs from their blowholes.

After dinner at a riverside rib shack, Colin decided to stop by Robyn's. The Lincoln didn't buck or skip anymore. The moon was up, everything green, almost magical. Illusion. The world, lit by the country club lights, was a leafy pastel. Colin rolled slowly so that an FM concerto would finish before he arrived. He was pleased he had chosen a little-traveled back road, but suddenly the Lincoln's headlights caught a tall man in an overcoat trying to climb into a dumpster. Colin slowed. The tall figure turned. Colin flicked on his high beams, then stopped in the middle of the road. For a moment, he did not realize what filled the windshield, then the bear left its foraging in the dumpster and took several steps on its hind legs. It just stood there, swayed from side to side, carved by the lights, like a mad and necessary thought. Moonlit shapes of trees gathered behind him. Dogs barked and he lowered himself to all fours and ran onto the fairway. Three dogs circled and yapped before he sent one flying with a single ferocious swipe, then broke through a thicket of bushes and disappeared. Stunned, Colin pulled to the roadside. Slowly, he got out, wondering if he really saw what he saw. The barking was distant now. He crossed the fence and walked into the small field. A fetid, rank smell rode the air. Sure enough. The dog lay on its side with three parallel blood stripes that started at the base of the neck and stopped at the rib cage. It lay absolutely still staring with one open eye at the moon. "God," he whispered. Excitement quickened inside him, pleasantly spreading its warmth.

The TV was still on, the sound mercifully down.
"I thought we were having dinner tonight."

"Did I say that?"

She looked him in the eye. "You're not *that* forgetful."

"Well, I don't know."

"Know what, what do you mean? What's the matter?"

Colin wasn't ready to tell her about the bear, and he wouldn't tell her about the TKE kid. He wanted to ask what Kirby's car was doing here last night, but somehow couldn't bring himself to do that either. "Nothing," he said.

"I called you a dozen times since you left in that huff."

"No huff, I was just restless."

"Anyway, I called and there was no answer."

Colin told her about putting new plugs in the Lincoln.

"Great." She threw her arms around him. "Guess what?"

"What?"

"I got us a video for tonight."

"Aren't you taking me for granted?"

She reached up and kissed him. "Why shouldn't I?"

Before he could stop himself, he said, "Because Kirby was here last night."

Her eyebrows rose in surprise, then she got a knowing smile. "You fool, Kirby was here for five minutes. He was actually looking for you. I made it clear I was busy. I've got to show you something," she said. With the remote, she rewound the tape. "This falls into 'Scenes We Like To See 'em Make.'" Lights from police cruisers flashed. The camera looked at upturned faces of neighbors. A uniformed man from Animal Control loaded a tranquilizer rifle. The bear looked down. There was a crack and in close-up a hot pink dart was visible on the bear's black haunch. It roared, then started to fall, but caught itself halfway down the tree. The picture bounced as the cameraman retreated to his car. A fat man tried to scale a cyclone fence. Robyn cackled. The bear disappeared into the dark. The reporter said that the bear would be followed until it fell asleep, then be loaded on a truck, and released far from town.

"They've probably got him by now."

Colin shook his head no. "I just saw him."

"You're joking. Where?"

"Over on Country Club Lane," he said.

"What, was he getting in a few midnight rounds?"

"Right."

"Mmmmm, very existential."

Colin went to the front porch and looked toward the halo of bright lights over the town. There was a lot of darkness beyond the lights and he was glad of it. The bear could be looking at him right now and knowing it made him feel the chill pimples standing on his forearms. Funny how the line kept coming back lately: *The readiness is all.* He thought about it in a different context. You ascertain lack of breath and pulse, open the airways, four ventilations, then . . . He was ready. At least he thought he was, but after he and Robyn watched the movie, after beers and small talk, Robyn said: "I think it's time for us to do something. I'm thinking we should live together. We can help each other a lot. You knew this was coming, didn't you?"

Knowing the importance of truth in affairs of the heart, Colin wisely lied. Across the street, he saw a match flare, disappear, and leave the glow of a cigarette that reminded him of that hot pink dart on the bear's flank. Reaching back with a snarl, the bear swept it away. "Let's do it," he said and kissed her. They looked at each other and kissed again, Colin feeling himself swept along, caught in the strong undertow of her touch.

Simple Misalignment

I run every day. My ex told friends almost nothing could stop me. Thanks to Gore-Tex, not even the rain. Jogging is good for certain problems. For the past week, I've been running longer distances. I escape completely or become absorbed with the whys, make decisions. My usual circuit ends at the Safeway parking lot. I stretch out, cool down, and sometimes grab a Diet Coke for the walk back. Today it's close to ninety degrees but clouds are on the build, blue-black, and rain might bring down the temperature, slowly, not like this wicked, quick-change flash I get from the arctic Safeway air. A cold drink is all I want, but once in the aisles, I'm reminded of needs, and not just bread alone. I'm considering a box of Cheerios when somebody says, "Hey, Tonto, long time no see."

Chuck. For six years, we taught at the same high school. Chuck quit after his divorce. A former tackle, well tanned, twin mirrors for eyes, he has gone through lots of changes. His weight is down and he wears the kind of youthful look that almost says: *I, ah, think I'll grab a few rays.*

"What's with the beard and shades?" I ask.

Chuck is six-four and looks down. "The only alternative to death, amigo, is change."

"Been watching talk shows, huh?"

"I'm into nutrition," he says.

I think of the old Groucho Marx show and tell myself, an audience of one, clichés will sooner or later lead to the secret word, *bottomline;* it will only be a matter of minutes before the duck descends.

A hefty polyester woman clashes her cart into a display stack of Pringles and sends tubes rolling in the aisle.

Chuck snuffs. "She's probably strung out on caffeine or sugar."

I ask why I haven't seen him on the tennis court lately.

He puts his palm to the small of his back and produces a wince. "Had to lay off—doctor's orders. Maybe a year, maybe for good."

"Really?"

"Better believe it, man. If you was smart, you'd knock off too."

"Why?"

"Lateral movement."

"So?"

"Worst thing in the world for the spine."

A young woman with a lovely face and delightful proportion maneuvers her cart past us; she is wearing white shorts and a blue Franz Liszt T-shirt. I say, "Franz, that ol' Hungarian, seems to be smiling. You wonder what he has at the back of his mind."

"Smoking," says Chuck. He hisses it. "She's smoking. See, see that? I almost punched out this smoker at the Wendy's salad bar."

My goose bumps are mountainous. I have to move, improve my circulation before I get frostbite. He follows and tells me about inconsiderate smokers, poisoning everyone else's air. "Let me share something with you."

Share. I can almost hear the quack of Groucho's duck. "OK, share," I say.

"You really going to eat that yogurt?"

"Why not?" I ask.

"It makes mucus, too much mucus—your cilia drown in that shit. They can't do their filtering number. Never mind the cholesterol."

I ask if that's what he wants to share.

"No, I was going to tell you about smoke. I used to go into bars for socialization purposes and—"

"Socialization? To pick up women, you mean."

He frowns, shakes his head; I vanish and reappear several times in the mirror lenses. "OK, to meet women," he says. "Anyway, no more. Too much smoke. All the studies say you might as well be smoking yourself."

"But, Chuck, weren't you a Marlboro man?"

"This is true. When I went to this guy about my back, I quit. He gave me confidence in myself, smoking cessation techniques. Plus hypnosis and acupuncture. Man, I went the whole detox route. No more substances."

"Did you go to an orthopedic man?"

His mouth winces, as if tasting diesel fuel. He says, "Well, at first I did, but those guys are a joke. They go after symptoms, never treat—his mouth rounds like a choirboy's when he says it—the Whole Person." Chuck is eating some kind of seeds, shaking them in his fist like a crapshooter. "Do me a favor," he says, "get rid of that yogurt and try some of these. Here."

I ask what they are.

"Don't worry, they're not peanuts—peanuts'll kill you. Read the studies. Farmers use all these pesticides for nematodes. You want nuts that are in trees."

"Thanks," I say. "I just ran six miles, I want something to drink."

"Ever try papaya juice? Really good for you."

I start walking again.

"Hey, I just want to share some information with you. Share. That's what it's all about. You still sore about the psycho?"

When Chuck was still at the high school, he coached baseball and worked as a guidance counselor. The year of his resignation, he put a number of outpatients from the state mental hospital into select classes without alerting teachers in question on the grounds they might object or not teach in a normal way. "Mainstreaming" was the thing. One of Chuck's experiments ("Hey, life is an experiment, right?") turned up in my class, acted goofy, and I lost control. There was a horrible scuffle when I finally had to eject him physically from the room.

Chuck says, "Hey, the kid didn't weigh a hundred pounds soaking wet."

"Sure," I say, "but crazy has something like a wind-chill factor with it."

He laughs. "You handled it OK. If I was still into substances, I'd buy, but—hey, I'll make it up to you. I've got something to show you later."

Anxious for another topic, I ask how his private counseling service is going. He makes a so-so gesture with his big mitt. Things take time. A little marriage and divorce work. But Amway is saving him. And somehow I feel saved by a fat man in Bermuda shorts who slips past eating a big candy bar with a yellow wrapper. He looks back at us sheepishly. Chuck says the guy's begging for a coronary, then turns the guns on me. He tells me I have deep frown lines, I'm squinting, look pale, tired. Do I know that I look hyper-tense? Probably too much sodium and not enough Vitamin C.

"I get plenty of sunshine."

"And plenty of salt," he says. His tone is accusing.

He has me—I love salt.

"Let me show you something," says Chuck. We go up the center aisle toward the last section where the vegetables are, and there at the entrance to the vegetable Eden is the angel in the Franz Liszt

T-shirt; cigarette between forked fingers, she is doing a few steps to an upbeat tune on the house Muzak, ready to choose between the Joy and Dawn. Lovely caramel skin and hair that is long and the color of honey. She is wearing a half smile and seems to give me a look. As we idle past, Chuck is going on about lactic acid and blood sugar. "You have no idea the kind of things a body craves."

"True," I say, looking at her, and know that when I get back to my apartment, I'll put on the famous B-minor sonata, lie down, and close my eyes.

"Still smoking," Chuck says in disgust.

The last aisle in the store is fruits and vegetables, cooler/crispers on both sides, bins for less perishable things in the center. "God, look at this," says Chuck. He moves along the bins, hovering, hefting cabbage and heads of endive, talking up the benefits of broccoli, asparagus ("Good for the kidneys"), spinach ("Popeye knew a good thing") and how you should eat them raw or make concoctions in your blender. He holds a big cauliflower in his palm and looks down thoughtfully as if addressing the skull of Yorick. "I'm about ready to do it," he says.

"What?" I ask. So many other people in the store are eating I suspect for a moment he intends to devour the cauliflower amidst all this garden color he is so intoxicated by.

"I'm going vegetarian," he says.

I nod, cock an ear, and look up for Groucho's duck.

"Not all at once," he says. "Taper off, clean myself out. Once you're off it, you can smell meat eaters."

"I must smell pretty bad," I say.

He ignores me. "Like, once you've kicked meat, you feel clean, more in touch with your body. You can almost hear your organs talking to each other. You know?"

"I can imagine."

"Once I was off it for a while and got myself in the situation where I ate meat just to be polite. Next time I won't compromise."

"Chuck, this is how fanatical religions start. Next it's eating codes and laws, two years at hard labor for chicken livers, the death penalty for pork chops, and on and on."

He shakes his head, drops the cauliflower, gives me his best disgusted look.

I ask if there aren't certain essentials you can't sufficiently get from anything but meat?

He shakes his head knowingly. "I've researched this thoroughly."

"I've heard that, ah, your quantum of wantum declines."

"If we were still in high school," he says, "that might be funny."

I agree. This is no laughing matter. My neck muscles are becoming tight. He looks me over and asks me to turn sideways. For some reason, I do. He makes a blade of his hand, puts it to his nose and squints, a kind of vertical salute. His diagnosis: I have a slouch. "How old are you?"

"Chuck, we were in the sixth grade together. Remember?"

He describes a set of symptoms and asks if any apply to me. I hate to admit it but most do. I hedge.

"Go like this," he says, extending his arms and touching his palms together. I look around. This chilly garden of fallen vegetables is deserted. "For God's sake," he says, "don't be so uptight. Good, that's it. See, your left arm is three inches shorter than your right. You get stiffness in your lower back, right?"

He's got me. My back is giving me trouble.

He feels my neck and slides thumb and forefinger down my spine. "You've probably got," he says, "a vertebral subluxation."

"A what?"

He repeats it. "A vertebral subluxation."

"Isn't that over in the shampoo aisle, next to the Herbal Essence?"

"Very funny. Hey, it's *your* back."

"So you think jogging is bad?"

"Bad? Worse thing in the world. I was preparing for a marathon, doing twelve miles a day before I found myself in traction. Get yourself a ten-speed bike—I did. Just as good for cardiovascular."

"What about weights?"

He stares.

"Worst thing in the world, huh?"

"Better believe it."

"But how do you keep your gut down, stay toned?"

Suddenly Chuck drops to the floor. "I'll show you. These are good for your back too. Palms under your buns and rock. Great for stomach. Ball player I know bet me he could do fifty." Chuck gets off the floor. "Never got past thirty. Get down, try a few."

Still deserted. Nobody has yet passed through this section. A tier of endive heads in the crisper is the only audience. I get to the floor. Chuck's bearded face hovers above, the mouth moving with instructions. I can see myself in his lenses struggling like a turtle. I'm straining to get a knee to my chin when the principal's secretary, Miss Hooks, looks down at me over her glasses, then disappears. Chuck, now free of the school, makes a remark about the eavesdropping business, just loud enough for her to hear.

"Wonderful," I say, getting to my feet.

Walking toward the checkout, past an old woman talking to the picture on a box of cat food, I see the Liszt lady again and give her a nod. As in the commercials, I see us running together along a beach with salt-white dunes, glassy breakers, just the two of us, hair fluffy and afloat. And it's suddenly hot again, a blanketing heat that is oddly welcome.

The big black lake of the parking lot is shimmering with warping curtains of hot air. Chuck is talking about his back man; a performer of miracles he is, but if I'm not too bad off, there is something that might make a trip to this healer unnecessary. The trunk of his old maroon Lincoln pops open: boxes of running shoes, sweat bands, cans of tennis balls, unstrung tennis and racketball rackets, and what appears to be dozens of wooden statues bagged in clear plastic. Chuck opens a bag and slides out one of these lathe-rounded hunks of stained wood for my closer inspection. It is a kind of rolling pin seemingly designed by somebody who has been an abuser of substances. Two opposed ebony cones taper toward each other, and at the narrow center are two cinnamon donuts some two inches apart. The idea, Chuck explains, is to lie on top of this "spinal aligner"—for such is it called—with the donuts on either side of the spinal column. Then you regulate pressure by adjusting your weight as you roll it from the small of the back to the neck. "They're great," says Chuck. "Unless you've got a serious subluxation, you'll feel great with this. Ten bucks."

Ten bucks. I figure if it doesn't help the back, I still have an interesting piece of sculpture.

"Don't pay me unless you decide to keep it," he says.

"What are these things?" At first look they seem to be half-finished ski boots. Four or five boxes.

"Big item," says Chuck. "Gravity boots. They go like hot cakes. Now, ah, they're good for your back too."

"Is that right?"

"Come on. Didn't you see *American Gigolo?*"

Now it clicks. I say yes and see Richard Gere hanging upside-down from a beam in his apartment.

"How do you use these things if you don't happen to live in an apartment with sturdy exposed beams?"

"You get a Doorway Gym." He reaches behind the boots and draws out a yard-long, silver bar bagged in tough plastic. "Ta da! You tighten it against your door frame and you're in business."

"Well."

"$8.95. Hey, for the back, it beats jogging. I read an article about it the other day."

"And the gravity boots?"

"These are the originals. Since the movie came out, the market's had a lot of plastic imitations."

"Fine, but how much?"

"$79.95."

I whistle.

"Forget that. For you, $65.00. And that's cost."

I ask what happens if you get stuck upside down. Chuck says you just grab your thighs and hand over hand to your ankles. No sweat. It doesn't sound convincing and for some reason my mind produces that famous picture of poor old Mussolini kicking his heels at heaven, so I decide to stick with the aligner; I put my foot up on his bumper and fish a ten from my running shoe wallet with the Velcro flap.

"Hey, now that's an item," says Chuck, squatting down to work the flap himself. "I ought to get a few."

"Probably sell like hot cakes," I say, thankful Chuck ignores my mockery.

He says, "You don't have to pay me. First, see if it works."

I press the ten into his Dockers pocket.

"Okay," he says. "Hey, if you got a buddy true and blue . . ."

"Fuck him," I say, finishing the old high school adage, "before he fucks you," and we just stand there looking at each other and laugh like hell, slowly tapering off.

"If the aligner doesn't work, see Dr. Kahn. He's in the Yellow Pages. Tell him I sent you. You'll feel like a kid again."

"Thanks."

"And try to give up that yogurt."

I say I will and walk across the parking lot that exits onto my street, not wanting to look back. The heat is wonderful. I'm sweating again. Once around the corner, I stop by a picket fence tangled with new roses, a side yard mountainous with lilac bushes, white peaks of bloom. The scent is delirious. Between two houses, I can see the parking lot. Chuck's car is still there, the trunk open. A small red sports car next to it. He is talking to the Franz Liszt woman. Her trunk is open too. They are standing close, facing each other. She is looking up. Chuck has taken off his sunglasses. Clouds are eating up the sun, billowing into the shapes of cauliflower and eggplant, squash and fans of celery. Suddenly I recall his remark about not going into bars anymore because of the smoke. But she is nodding her head and seems to be reaching out to him. She is touching her palms. I'm certain one of her arms is shorter than the other. But that's not the problem. The scent of lilac is unbearable and I back away wondering if Chuck can save her from cigarettes, the world of smoke and fire. A guy in a tan summer suit moves along the shaded sidewalk with a hint of destination in his stride, whistling, newspaper under his arm. He grows small and turns the corner. I'm in no big hurry. As I saunter along, it comes to me that Groucho's duck never descended. So send not to ask for whom the duck quacks . . .

And that's the bottomline.

Palliatives

The concourse at Sky Harbor was thick with travelers and roared like the jets that lumbered back and forth in taxi lanes beyond the plate glass. Check-in counters had long lines. Lounges were full, people standing. Fourth in line from the counter, Alan was trying to keep alive images of monks robed in gold from the last few months, trying to breathe deeply and slowly, keep faith with certain precepts learned in the mountains. Control was everything. A guy with a red tie seated left of the counter angrily stared. Alan knew one's appearance could always ignite something— that's the way this country was. In India nobody would have paid any mind to his rumpled white shirt, shaved head, and gold earring. Or his unshaven face, puffy with that sleepless look of the jet-lagged.

Too many time zones. Leaving Bombay, he felt good. The glary tin sheet that was the Arabian Sea disappeared when the plane banked eastward, then the emerald jungle disappeared below clouds. But neither mantra nor his established practice of zazen helped much with endless airborne hours. His legs got nervous, then numb. Finally he swallowed ten milligrams of Xanax and slept, but just before the plane landed in Hawaii, he popped awake in a chilly vagal sweat. Giardia? The in-flight meal? Trying to breathe deeply and calm his stomach, he found himself staring at the T-shirt of a kid in the aisle; it showed a smiling man with a fishing rod in one hand and what appeared to be a moth in the other. He read, "The Way To A Man's Heart Is Through His Fly," gagged, and made a grab for the sick bag that was not entirely successful.

The Asian flight attendant seemed genuinely kind and provided him with a plastic bag for his soiled and reeky shirt. His seatmate, a woman with red hair and freckles, began to get green. Others aimed sour looks. In the cramped lavatory, Alan changed into the only thing he had in his carry-on bag: a wrinkled white shirt with a yellow curry stain on the pocket. *The wind collects the clouds, and the wind drives them away again,* Alan recalled. He tried to tell himself that appearance was nothing, but the motley image of himself kept swimming to mind.

Inching toward a check-in counter, he was trying to focus on something else, trying to visualize the saintly Tibetan face of Golpen Rinpoche. The line was long, departure time close. Passengers were tsking and complaining about flight delays. A woman in the next line coughed. She had a lovely face. A cool blonde in a white summer skirt and jacket, long hair. She was beautiful until she began to talk to the black woman at the counter. She said in a hissy voice that the delay was unacceptable. She flipped her gold hair back, jade studs in her ears. Her husband was a lawyer. She wanted some kind of compensation. The black woman said that the East Coast had been fogged in until nearly eleven o'clock. The classy woman's face became red and twisted: "I have been *terribly* inconvenienced, I have *missed* my connecting flights, I—"

"Ma'am, if you would care to read the back of your ticket, you will see we are not responsible for any delays caused by weather."

"You people—I am sick of this fucking attitude."

The black woman looked up from her computer screen and very calmly said, "I do not have to take this kind of abuse—"

"You fucking well do, I want to speak to your supervisor, right now!"

The black woman returned her gaze to the screen and continued typing.

An airline representative with silver wings on his black lapel arrived and took the blonde aside. She was tapping her foot and shaking her head no, no, no.

Behind Alan, an attaché clicked down on its metal studs. A man's voice said, "Look at that faggot."

Another said, "Swings his butt like a woman."

A woman's voice over the public address system said, "Will passenger Gustavo Maria Jiminez please join your party in the baggage claim area."

Alan breathed deeply. The voice behind him said, "Maybe that was Maria we just saw." They laughed.

Alan couldn't bring himself to turn and face the men behind him. He imagined cowboy hats and bola ties attached to the voices.

Again the voice on the public address said: "Will passenger Gustavo Maria Jiminez please report to your party in the baggage claim area."

"Party? Hey, I wonder if *we* could go to that party?"

They snorted. "Buncha beaners doin' their sisters."

Alan attended to his careful breathing: *What is the Buddha?* The man with the red tie left his seat by the window to talk to the airline rep behind the counter. Finally, he blew out his cheeks, flung up his hand, and returned to his seat. *The Buddha is a dung beetle.*

After Alan had his ticket processed, he looked around for an empty chair. He felt lucky to find one next to two slim women with wire glasses who were laughing. He tried not to look around, but when he did, the guy with the red tie was staring at him from a distance of twenty feet. What was his problem? He seemed about thirty, Alan's age, but with a darker skin, handsome. He wore loose white trousers, a blue oxford shirt, and a red paisley tie. One of the women with wire-glasses mocked a TV ad, "With Degree, when your body temperature rises, more deodorant protection is automatically released."

"'Automatically' is the operative word," said the other.

"That's progress!" They both giggled.

An announcement said they were now ready to board the last fifteen rows of the plane. As passengers began to stampede toward the jet bridge, one of the women with wire-glasses turned to Alan and laughed. "Do they really think," she said, "the plane is going to leave without them?"

Alan smiled and said, "The mind is a monkey."

The women looked at each other and laughed. An American Airlines 757 lumbered past the window. The desert runways were glaring white, sun banging off the silver skins of the aircraft. Alan stared at heat-shimmered fuel trucks and baggage trains. *Hide yourself in the middle of the flames.* Alan silently made the words with his lips. He saw the old face of Golpen Rinpoche with his kind eyes, the ears comically large, in his maroon and gold robes, and it brought him quiet. After sitting zazen for a long stretch that was beginning to seem less and less long, he would climb the path from his bungalow to the hermit center for his meeting with the Master who would ask simple questions about entanglement and pure mind. Then Alan would walk, fingering his beads, just concentrating on what he was doing until the doing became pure, and sometimes didn't. Clouds would drift across snowy ramparts of Kanchenjunga high above. Below were the rooftops of Dharamsala and children's kites holding steady above them. But there were also walks on the tea plantation where you were by yourself, fingering your beads. One evening, near dusk, one of the snowy peaks showed itself briefly. A thunking sound of someone chopping wood deep in the valley came up with a scatter of laughter. A raven cawed and sailed out of sight. Everything became quiet as a still-life. Then he noticed it was very cold; he tried not to mind it, but finally hurried down to his bungalow.

Before Alan could take his seat, a woman struggled to hoist a bag that was clearly too large for the overhead compartment. A line of people waited behind her. A flight attendant with coppery hair offered to check the bag. "I can't," said the woman. "I'm going to Paris. I need it with me."

The flight attendant said it was obvious the bag wouldn't fit, and the aisle needed to be cleared so other passengers could be seated. "I'd be very happy to check that for you."

Reluctantly the woman handed over the bag and muttered an obscenity under her breath.

Finally Alan took his seat on the aisle. The middle and window were already occupied by a couple who would be, he thought, about the age of his parents, if they were still alive. "We're the Ralstons from Raleigh," the woman said with a smile. She had the beginning of dowager's hump that made Alan think of osteoporosis. Mr. Ralston reached over to shake hands. He wore rimless glasses and a gold neck chain of square links, a spread-winged eagle pendant. A big man with red-threaded eyes. Alan gave his name and said he too was from Raleigh.

"Not originally," said Mr. Ralston, who had the window seat.

"That's true," Alan admitted. "Ohio."

"I'll bet I can guess your age," Mrs. Ralston said, and did.

"Now it's my turn," said Alan.

"Don't you dare!" She laughed and her eyes squeezed into slits. Plum lipstick extended the outlines of her meager lips. Her color was good and she looked a bit younger than her husband, though she seemed to have given up her struggle with weight.

"Are you all right?" asked Mrs. Ralston.

Alan apologized for his appearance and said he had gotten sick.

"That's a nice earring," said Mrs. Ralston.

Alan said thank you, taking out *Peaks and Lamas,* which he had been reading before Hawaii.

"Claude thinks all kinds of things about men with earrings and tattoos." Her skin was florid and her eyes suggested some inner amusement. "Not me, I take people like they are."

Claude's complexion was gray. He was looking through the window at the runway and said, "That's not true. Erma, please don't start."

Alan didn't want to talk about himself, so he asked, "Are you from Phoenix?"

"Shame on you," Mrs. Ralston said, "We just told you we're the Ralstons from Raleigh."

Alan apologized. "I'm a bit disoriented."

"We just came out here to Phoenix for a funeral."

Alan apologized again.

"Well, Julia was only twelve."

Alan nodded.

"My sister was destroyed."

Alan didn't know what to say, the vocabulary of condolence was so limited. "I'm sure she was."

"Such intelligent eyes, beautiful hair."

Mr. Ralston said, "She was spoiled. She'd bite the hand that fed her."

"The trouble," said Mrs. Ralston, "with dogs and cats is that we outlive them and have to go on alone."

"Nastiest bitch I ever seen."

Alan shifted in his seat, but just as he was about to read, Erma said, "Do you have relatives in Phoenix here?"

Alan said he didn't.

"Then how did you get here?"

"Hawaii."

"Oh that must be paradise."

Alan explained that Hawaii was the second stop, that he had come from Bombay to Tokyo, Tokyo to Hawaii."

"Why'd you do that?"

"I was in India."

"Oh," said Mrs. Ralston, smiling and nodding. "How long?"

"About a year."

Mr. Ralston leaned forward and said, "That's just wall-to-wall beggars, isn't it?"

"See how he is?" said Erma.

"It's a fact," said Mr. Ralston. "I read it. We was poor but proud oncet upon a time, but these people will cut their kid's hands off, or gouge out an eye so they's more pitiful-like for begging."

"I can't argue with him. He reads fact books. I prefer fiction," she said, showing Alan a Sidney Sheldon novel with a lurid cover.

"And they all worship cows." He shook his head. "Buddhists," he snorted.

"Hindus," said Alan.

"Same difference."

Mrs. Ralston said, "Some people *do* get carried away with these different religions."

"Mormons are worst of all," said Mr. Ralston. "They're knocking on your door all the time. They're against coffee, beer, and tobacco. Where would our state be without tobacco?"

"True," said Mrs. Ralston.

"But they go ahead and have a dozen wives. Sex maniacs is what they are. They practiced selective breeding, just like Nazis. Brigham Young hand-picked the strongest and best looking for breeding stock. Blond hair and blue eyes. I read it in a book."

The captain announced that they had a problem with a latch

on the cargo door, and since the delay would be slight, there was no point in having passengers deplane. The pilot said the delay would be fifteen minutes, but it had gone well beyond that now. The Arizona sun was heating up the cabin. Alan got out of his seat and went to the back of the plane. "Nervous legs," he explained to two flight attendants in the galley, wishing he was dressed differently.

"No problem," said one. She was trim, in a black skirt and white blouse with a red scarf, and had coppery hair, a lovely smile. The other had hair that was very blonde and wore a lot of make-up. Alan asked her where they were from. The one with the coppery hair said she was from Atlanta. Her nameplate said, "Lee Anne." The blond was from Wilmington. Alan enjoyed hearing the broad mellow vowels again. He found it hard not to sneak looks at the one with coppery hair. She didn't pluck her eyebrows and had smooth natural skin. She was talking to another passenger, a guy in a light suit and yellow tie, telling him she had been saving money to open a restaurant, and the kitchen in her place would be a lot cleaner than this galley. They both laughed. Another year and she would be able to settle down.

"Pardon me." It was the guy with the red tie, and he ran his eyes over Alan before saying, "How much longer do you expect we are going to be made uncomfortable?" His accent was British.

Lee Anne smiled and said, "Just a moment, I'll see," and picked up the phone. She relayed the question to the cockpit then said, "The captain apologizes for the delay, but it won't be much longer."

"Apologies is it? I'm bloody well sick of apologies."

"I might could get you something to drink if you'd like," she smiled.

"You *might could?* Then I'll take a neat gin and some ice."

When Lee Anne stooped and hauled open a deep metal drawer for ice, he looked at Alan, then the guy in a suit. "Might could," he sneered. "This delay is going to completely bollocks my connections. I've got a mate waiting for me at Gatwick."

"Here you are, sir," she said.

When he turned and left without a word, she flashed a big smile: "He could have at least said, 'Cheers.'"

"Lee Anne, my name is Lee," said the guy in the suit and tie. He laughed. "Really, I didn't make that up." He shook hands with everyone, Alan too. "Those Brits, I'll tell you," he said. "One day I was in Paris during a terrible downpour. I shared this shop doorway with a Brit for about fifteen minutes. Very nice conversation. We talked the whole time about this, that, and the other thing. Toward the end, he told me that English and American are two entirely different languages. Can you imagine that?" He shook his head. "Entirely different."

Alan once more opened his book. Out of the corner of his eye, he could see that the cloudscape at Mr. Ralston's window had tempting towers and fantastic shapes, but he resisted turning his head to look more directly past his two seatmates. To himself, he whispered *Kanchenjunga*. When lunch was served, however, it was impossible to avoid conversation.

"What kind of work do you do?" Mrs. Ralston asked.

"Hospital work."

"Really? Our son works at Duke with lavatory animals."

Alan almost laughed. He said, "Does he have a research grant?"

"No, he just takes care of them. Are you an orderly?"

"I'm a med student, or was."

"That's just what our Dickey wants to be, but—"

"But," said Mr. Ralston, "he's only white. Med schools got these quotas. So many Japs, so many Indians, blacks, Mexicans, Martians, and all the rest."

"And women," said Alan.

"Yes, and *women*."

"A question of fairness," said Alan.

Mrs. Ralston said to her husband, "Honey, he *knows* that. He's a *medical* student after all." She turned to Alan. "What med school were you at?"

"Carolina."

"How nice!"

"When will you finish?"

"I'm not sure."

"You *are* going to finish, I hope."

"I'm not sure."

"What do your parents say?"

Alan explained that his parents had died in an accident.

Mrs. Ralston had a stricken look. "I'm sorry."

"It happened when I was much younger."

"But, Lord, you can do so much good as a doctor," said Mrs. Ralston. "Sorry, that's just the mother in me talking."

After the flight attendant brought coffee, she said, "What were you doing in India?"

Alan took a deep breath. There was no way he could explain the second part of his trip, the Himalayas and the monastery, so he said that he had felt overdosed with school and along came a chance to go to India and do some medical field work.

"I wouldn't know one end of India from the other, but—"

"Why bother to know it?" muttered Mr. Ralston.

"—where were you?"

"Calcutta. It's hotter than the Himalayas. I was at a center established by the order of nuns that Mother Teresa belongs to, Little Sisters of the Poor. Do you know about them?"

Mrs. Ralston knew. "She won the, ah—"

"Nobel Peace Prize."

"That's right. Yes. Did you ever meet her?"

"Oh yes. She works with the sick and dying like everyone else."

"But what's her angle?" asked Mr. Ralston.

"Claude, honey, if—"

"Live long enough and you learn everybody has an angle, everybody."

"Is that right?" said Alan, knowing that answering Mr. Ralston would mean personal failure, but control slipped away. "An old Chinese monk said that 98 percent of what we do is for the self, but the surprise is that there is no self."

Mr. Ralston snorted, "That don't amount to spit on a griddle . . . Chinese! If Dickey ever goes off the deep end like 'at—" But he didn't finish the sentence.

Mrs. Ralston said, "What was Calcutta like?"

Alan looked at the seatback in front of him. All he had to do was close his eyes and India was back: sidewalk campfires and sleeping bodies, blue-black cows, buses and trains crammed with bodies, people even riding on roofs, heat and dust, parched lips, droves of bicycles and motor scooters, rickshaw wallahs, fakirs and babus, the scent of incense and kitchen smells of ginger, curry, and the sweetish rot of vegetation and burning garbage, cow dung, nightsoil and urine, smells he had never smelled before, and the look of women in bright saris, their caste marks and nose studs. One evening he stood on a dirt road in the blue smoky air before a grove of creaking bamboo that seemed to be whipping the clouds along. He just stood there looking at traveling clouds, listening to monkeys chitter in the trees. An old man approached, his eyes living opals, did a namaste, and continued on. India wasn't just a different country, it was a different world, another dimension of reality.

"Well?"

"I'm sorry. I was just thinking about how to answer that. It's not a postcard—that's for sure. There is a lot of squalor, a lot of beauty too. They're inseparable and heighten each other. The poor have few illusions."

Mr. Ralston laughed the phlegmy laugh of a smoker. "That's a hot one," he said, unable to stop coughing.

"Excuse me," said Alan, and left his seat.

The flight attendant named Lee Anne said, "How's those nervous legs?"

"Still nervous," said Alan. He told her how long he had been flying and where he had come from. "That's fascinating," she said. "I'd love to go to India." She said he had her beat by a mile in terms of continuous crossing of time zones. Her flying was limited to the States, and most of the time not even coast to coast. Alan listened to her talk. She was lovely. He'd rather stand here for the next three hours than return to his seat. Alan turned. Lee, the guy with the suit and tie, was back. He told Alan that time passed more quickly and enjoyably when people spoke to one another, but Lee seemed to do all the speaking, telling Alan about his plans to open a golf resort in the mountains near Asheville. He knew many famous people who would make it fly, Sean Connery for one, Sigourney Weaver for another. Suddenly his expression changed. The Brit with the red tie was back, his eyes reddish and glassy. He told the flight attendant he was very unhappy with the service. He said that he had left a day early from California so that his mother could stay the night in Raleigh and be rested for the flight to London. Lee Anne said they could perhaps rewrite the ticket in Raleigh. She pulled out a schedule and told him another flight was leaving Raleigh two hours later and would bring him into Manchester at a reasonable time.

"Reasonable time—that's a bloody joke. I don't *want* to go to Manchester."

"You could take the train—"

"We were to have been met by certain persons at Gatwick."

"The airline would be happy to phone these people about your change of plans."

"But that would inconvenience *them*."

Alan wondered what he wanted. She was offering help, but he was bent on something else.

"If you have any suggestions, I'd be more than happy—"

"I'm bloody disgusted with this airline. This is not the first time I've been buggered by them."

"I'm very sorry. Have you written any letters of complaint? I could give you the address."

"Don't bother—I've written."

"And?"

"Palliatives."

She smiled. "I don't know what you mean."

"Palliatives," he said slowly, pronouncing each syllable. "Perfectly good word." Then, mocking her accent, he said, "You *might could* look it up, learn somethin', dahlin."

Alan asked himself if a puppy dog had a Buddha nature. He watched the man named Lee lean forward and clear his throat. He said, "You know what they say, don't you? 'The best laid schemes of mice and men gang aft a-gley.'"

"I beg your pardon," said the Brit.

Lee repeated the line.

"What are you talking about?" he snapped.

"Burns."

"I've been *burned* all right."

"No, the Scottish poet, Robert Burns. An educated fellow like you should know a famous line like that." Then mimicking the man's British accent, Lee said, "But I expect you could look it up, learn something, ay mate?"

The other attendant who had been listening laughed.

"This don't concern you, so whyn't you just piss off?"

"Why don't you just have another pal-li-a-tive"—Lee said the last word slowly, one syllable at a time—"of the Beefeater variety?"

"Maybe you'd like to try me, mate."

Alan sensed a punch would be thrown, but just as their hands were coming up, a guy with a cowboy hat waiting for the lavatory stepped between them and said, "Gentlemen, gentlemen, let's chill it, hunh?"

"Good idea," said Lee Anne. To Alan, she whispered, "Please go back to your seat," her face pleading, not commanding.

Alan's scalp itched and his heart pounded. Mrs. Ralston leaned over and whispered to him. She wondered if he would be willing to change seats with her husband. "He's had some problems with his bladder and he sometimes needs to use the facilities in a hurry. I just don't want to have to wake you in case you fall asleep."

"That will be fine," he said, and after Mr. Ralston left for the lavatory, Alan settled into the window seat and looked out. Daylight was leaving. They were flying into the dark. Faint stars appeared in the fading blue. Mrs. Ralston said, "He's all bark and no bite. He just seems more and more, you know, flustrated by his physical problems."

It took him a moment to realize she was talking about her husband. Alan said he might be hyper tense. Tension, Alan could feel it himself, but he could control it too. Tempo had something to do with tension. His reflexes and his pulse had been speeding up since he left the mountains to adjust to the tempo of cities and crowds. The mountain tempo he had been living in for the past two months was far slower. His pulse had been barely fifty beats per minute. He'd be afraid to read it now.

"Do you think that's why he goes to the bathroom so often?"

"No, that could be prostatitis. Has he seen a doctor?"

"He's afraid to go, afraid of surgery."

"They can shrink the prostate now with a drug. Surgery might not be necessary. But I don't know, I'm just a student. He needs to see a urologist."

Mrs. Ralston didn't seem to be toying with him any longer. The amusement was gone from her eyes. When her husband returned, Alan opened his book, but found it hard to read. He thought about Golpen Rinpoche and could still see those beautiful Tibetan faces. He wondered if white Western faces could possibly be as attractive to them, as theirs were to him. In his hut, through the translator, the Master said more than once, *The wind collects the clouds, and the wind drives them away again.* You could drive them away was what he meant. His seatmates were asleep. Mr. Ralston's hands were folded on his belly. Alan looked at them carefully. He noticed the finger clubbing, the corrugation of the nail, the bulbous thickening at the turned down tip, the absence of any pinkness, the fatal gray. It was the classic look he had learned in his second year of Physical Diagnosis. Dr. Longman had it himself and invited the students to come up and examine his fingers. Laughingly, he said to the students, "These are the kind of fingers you don't want to have," and spelled out the implications: varying degrees of heart and lung disease. Mr. Ralston's clubbing was pretty severe. Alan took a deep breath. Bladder was the least of his problems. Alan felt sorry for him. Her too. He thought of his parents, what was beyond him, and what wasn't. Town lights far below like strings of galaxies. *The mind is a monkey.* He formed the words with his lips to savor them, though he didn't say them out loud. He could see the stupas and great reclining Buddha at Polonnaruwa. The huge empty face, a subtle stone smile and haunting look that has seen everything and accepts. It was uncanny. There would always be guys with red ties, of course, but that was no reason they had to exist. He reclined his seatback, began to breathe deeply, closed his eyes, and waited for clouds to slide from the snowy peaks of Kanchenjunga.

Costly Habits

Kurt was running out of things to do and clacked about the house like a bean in a matchbox. From the kitchen window, he peeked at the trap under the oak, its new wire glinting with promise. These gray squirrels had a way of landing on his roof with a slap, a sharp sound that was close to personal insult. Or they would seem to study him as they did now from nearby branches. Shoe polish in hand, he counted six before the hospital helicopter came low overhead and sent them scattering.

On the top step of the porch, with a dime, he levered open a can of black polish. The lid was shiny as a mirror inside. Kurt could see his dark hair, parted as if with a straight edge. Spitting on the folded rag, he dabbed polish, and rubbed it carefully into the leather of his tasseled loafers, one section at a time—something he did every other day before putting on a starchy white shirt. Shoes lasted longer, like anything else, if you took care of them.

The hum of roller-bladers lifted his attention. Gliding, holding hands, they shifted to a closed position, the boy dropping the girl into a tango-like dip, then sweeping her upright into a fluid turn. She had a lovely face, glistening black hair, long legs. Both wore headphones and moved gracefully to the same music, as if in a dream.

A blue jay jeered. Kurt worked furiously on the loafer. If he could get rid of the squirrels and quit cigarettes, things would be better. Cigarettes might even have cost him his job. Joan was right to hate his smoking. There had been no scene, no angry words—it wasn't their style. The school year done, Joan simply left him a note. She had taken Alicia to visit her parents a few towns away. That was two weeks ago, a week after his name appeared on the layoff list, but he hadn't told her yet. *Downsizing*—a tidy, clever word.

Across the street, shirtless and tanned up, Sonny was trimming holly that screened his porch. Kurt could see the new yin-and-yang tattoo on his shoulder, the blond ponytail wagging back and forth. Trimmings lay in a row where they would turn brown before Sonny got around to piling them at the curb for city collection. Kurt knew his routine. Sonny had owned the brick federal for three years and begun many projects, but rarely finished any. Sometimes he didn't weed his lawn, and soon it was covered with dandelion clocks. The prevailing southwest wind meant Kurt's weeding was for naught. Worse, Joan hated herbicides. But winsome Sonny, or his wife, Angela, would often cross the street to admire and ask advice, and Kurt would oblige with elaborate tips about shears, centipede, bermuda, and nutrient spikes—tips that were always ignored.

He squinted against glare. What was Sonny up to now? Juggling tennis balls, entertaining kids next door. The guy could never stay on task. But Joan liked his wacky charm, his ability to discuss politics and ideas, his knowledge of food and wines, his gusty enthusiasms. To Kurt, Sonny seemed a born loafer. Where did he get the money for that house with its gentle gables and dormers? He worked as a waiter, mostly on weekends, and for the rest had his face in a book. Angela was a part-time student and an aerobics instructor at the Athletic Club. But they had a powerboat, and Sonny always had weed. Kurt suspected he was involved in dope, was picking up offshore parcels for a profit. *Christ, you judge everyone,* Joan had said. Maybe Sonny was just one of these trust-fund brats. Kurt somehow thought his parents lived up North, in Scarsdale, where that diet doctor was murdered, the woman who did it out of jail now and peddling a book, collecting a bundle for film rights. Everyone had a scam.

Kurt had waxed the Taurus and showered. Arm weary, he stood at the window and saw how the car roof mirrored the trees. Except for an occasional slap of shingles, the quiet seemed magnified. None of the Vivaldi and Mozart that Joan listened to while grading student papers. Or Alicia humming over her coloring book. And none of Tucker's meows—he was gone with Alicia. Kurt had hopes the gray would be a squirrel killer, but Tucker turned out to be a big coward.

The bells of St. Ignatius rang a distant summons. Kurt was in no mood. Father Al's sermons were weak as drinks at the Dock House, except when he got passionate about pledges for a rec center. And the new church roof wasn't even paid for yet! Al had no more fiscal sense than the goddamned government. Just back from a stretch in Mexico, he had learned enough Spanish now to be able to bore the illegals in their own language. Kurt disliked foreign languages, especially in schools or church. His own grandfather spoke only German, and Kurt was never sure what in hell he was saying unless his mom was there to translate. But last night he had a dream and, except for his grandfather's gibberish—which seemed an attempt to tell Kurt something terribly important—the dream was a beautiful and seamless thing, full of cousins and the fun of building a towering tree house where, finally, they could see for miles. Nothing in Kurt's waking life seemed to form such a coherent whole these days. A moment here, a moment there.

Longing for a cigarette to go with his coffee, Kurt put down *Money* and went to the window. A timer had started his backyard sprinklers. He watched them slinging chains of water on the brilliant grass, then noticed the trapdoor of the shiny Havahart was closed. But instead of the frenetic back-and-forth of a squirrel, there was a flash of blue.

It was a jay. He knelt on the grass. The bird was the same blue as the hydrangea in Sonny's yard. Angela had arranged a bouquet when Kurt and Joan were last there for dinner, the night Sonny held forth about drawing. He was going to take courses because, self-taught, he knew little about composition. Copy was all he could do, like the painstaking kilim prayer rug, in colored inks, he had framed. Joan crooned over the detail. Kurt suspected you had to be stoned for that kind of concentration.

Joan said, "I've always wanted to draw and paint."

"Why not?" said Sonny. "I think it was Mallarmé who said, 'Le monde existe pour qu'on puisse le mettre dans une peinture.'"

Joan had studied French and knew what he said, but Kurt froze, played with the champagne cork, made it roll in wobbly little circles under the rounds of hydrangea bloom. Drawing—now she would have even less time to unclutter the house. Finally Kurt said, "Waiting on tables pay enough for the tuition and art supplies?" He said it jokingly. Sonny responded with a laugh and asked why Kurt disapproved. Back home, Joan said he had been rude.

Kurt sighed deeply. "Whatever."

"Did you notice that Sonny's face looked puffy?"

"No, but I noticed his new tattoo that's not even a picture. Ponytail, earring, tattoo." He snorted. "What's he trying to do, bring back the 60s?"

Joan, as if nobody had spoken, said, "His face seems swollen."

"He eats too much."

"No, that's the point. He eats like a bird."

"You're hot for him."

"Are you crazy? What's the matter with you?"

He lifted the trapdoor. The jay squawked and disappeared in the green shade. He reset the trap and put a handful of sunflower seeds on the trigger pan, then remained on his knees, staring at nothing.

A guy had barricaded himself in the Starlight Motel and was armed with a shotgun. The camera panned the front of the complex. Cops in black caps and jumpsuits scurried with automatic weapons. The newswoman told the camera that a mental health patient was holed up behind her. He was on the phone, with negotiators, asking to see his estranged wife and promising to commit suicide once he had seen her, no longer be a nuisance to anyone.

"Great," said Kurt to the screen, "Save everyone a lot of money."

Finally he came out with his hands up. Officers charged up the stairway, shoved him against the wall, and handcuffed him. The newswoman said the man was depressed because he was unemployed and had stopped taking his medication. Final footage showed a cop put his hand on the man's head and gently squash him into the back of a squad car.

Kurt quickly stabbed some numbers. "Hi, it's Kurt. Is Joan there? I'm fine, thanks . . ." Kurt could hear a TV in the background. Joan's parents were news junkies. When Joan came to the phone, he did his Bogart: "Listen, sweetheart, I'm barricaded in a room at the Starlight Motel. I'm armed and dangerous. Now, if you and the kid don't come to see me, it's curtains. I'll have to give myself an enema with this high-powered water pistol . . ." Using his own voice, he said, "Did you see the evening news?"

"You're hopelessly childish."

"I thought Sonny said any idiot could grow up and be responsible, but it took real talent to remain childish?"

"*Innocent* is the word he used."

"I heard another Sonny story today. Sonny gives the busboy at the Bistro a ride. Kid told me there's this awful stink. They open the trunk and find a dead cat. Then Sonny remembers. Miz Marsden, the old lady at the corner asked Sonny for help. Her cat, ol' Stonewall, had died. Sonny, of course, says yes, he'll take care of it, and forgets about the cat in the trunk. Ol' Sonny, he's quite a guy."

This was an absurd tale, with only a grain of truth, but ever since he entertained Joan's parents, easy gigglers, with anecdotes about Sonny, he couldn't quit. Sonny had become a character, and Kurt had only just discovered the pleasures of fabrication.

But Joan didn't laugh.

"You don't believe me? What am I hearing between the lines? Oh, I know. Shame on me—he's a very *giving* person. Is that it?"

"Yes, he gives you opportunity to feel superior."

Brushing his teeth in the mirror, Kurt still looked strange to himself without his beard, even though he cut it off long ago. The two couples had been having drinks at the Dock House when, as usual, Sonny made a definitive statement: *For some, a beard neither conceals nor reveals.* Even though Sonny was taking potshots at Republicans—just to taunt him, it seemed—and mocking a convicted born-again felon, Kurt wondered whether the comment applied to him. So he let a week go by, then shaved his beard, leaving a mustache for a few days, then shaved that too. He was thirty-seven. His teeth were very white. He was good looking. He had a first home in a once-elegant neighborhood on the comeback, in the historic district, one block from the waterfront. A systems analyst, he had a good income and would soon be back to work. Joan and Alicia would return.

The talk show host had seven couples seated in front of the camera. Each partner was exposing something unacceptable about the other. Kurt had heard tell of these programs, but, working, he never had a chance to see one, and now would never admit to Joan that he had. At first he felt vaguely guilty, then better, better because he never had the urge to wear Joan's panties, had not had an affair with her sister, never made Joan pick up after him (quite the contrary), wasn't obese, a closet drinker, a porno junkie, nose-picker, or shoplifter. Feeling better about himself, but vaguely like a voyeur, he hit the remote and the screen went black. He was, however, a smoker, but trying to quit.

Slowly, in his Taurus, Kurt followed two girls on roller blades. Both had smooth bronze skin, wore headbands and spandex bicycle shorts. One had long blonde hair. Kurt almost ran into them as they came whipping out of the Kappa house driveway and skated in the middle of the road. The girls were headed for the promenade—what Sonny called "ego alley." Kurt turned into his driveway, still seeing the lovely bottom of the blonde, but cheat on Joan—that was another thing he didn't do.

The Dock House had an upper verandah and outside seating, white tablecloths, candles in jars with plastic nets, and college kids in safari shorts working as waiters. You could drink outside and watch boats slide by or roller-bladers cutting figures, but Kurt favored the air-conditioning. Two dug-in drinkers down at the end of the bar sat behind change, car keys, cigarettes and lighters.

Wolfie was the bartender, a big guy with a wide flat face who spoke in a confiding way out of the corner of his mouth. He set down Kurt's gin and tonic and said in almost a whisper, "You need to talk to an employment counselor, do some networking. Support groups are the thing. I was there, man, I know what you're feeling like, like it's *your* fault, like you have no real worth. Before I got this job, I made lists, know what I mean?"

Kurt didn't.

"Every day you make a list, scratch off items as you complete each task, any little thing like emptying the garbage, washing your car. You have a sense of accomplishment. It's, like, the feeling of time wasted that gets to you, know what I mean?"

Kurt sipped his drink and nodded, looking at the red candles on the verandah that reminded him of church, Father Al and the Mexicans.

Wolfie continued, "This way you're in touch, you're the master, working your way toward a whole new reality. One thing at a time." Wolfie ran the rag over the dark wood of the bar. "You, ah, getting your résumé around?"

"Sure. E-mail, the net, bulletin boards."

Wolfie said, "Something will open up."

"Yeah, a black fucking hole."

"You playing any golf?"

"Wolfie, Joan's taken off, I've got no work, golf is the furthest—"

"Wait." Wolfie's face lit up. He told Kurt he had an idea. "I know this guy with a new software company. I'm supposed to play golf with him. You make the foursome, casually talk turkey, hey, something might happen!"

Kurt said thanks. But taking advice from a bartender—Christ, who would he be listening to next? Wolfie flashed his big canines. "Let me try to set it up, OK? Meanwhile, hit the driving range, this guy's good."

Kurt stood at the window, phone to his ear, listening to Joan and watching a squirrel, a fat one, come head first down the pecan tree. Once on the ground, it stood on hind legs, exposing a white belly and throat. "Joan, I'm her father. I'm allowed visitation."

"You sound like a soap. This is the first time you even mentioned her."

"Well, how about her spending Saturday with me?"

Joan said, "Fine."

One foot at a time, the squirrel moved toward the trap, thick brush tail straight out. "Have you, ah, been to a lawyer by any chance?"

Joan sighed. "Are you getting any exercise besides jumping to conclusions?"

With maddening slowness, the squirrel reached the wire.

Kurt said, "Well, I don't know what to think."

"That's up to you, but thinking instead of reacting would be a start."

The squirrel jumped on top of the trap and sat. "So, you're not coming back because *I* need to think about things."

"Partly, but I told you I need some space for a while."

"*I* don't give you space?"

Joan said nothing. The squirrel dropped again to the ground and stuck its head into the opening. Kurt whispered, "Come to Papa."

Joan said, "Who's there with you?"

"Nobody. You said *I* don't give you space."

"You're being argumentative. The quarrel ought to be with yourself."

"You sound like our neighbor, the deep thinker across the street." Kurt waited. Something spooked the squirrel. Now he seemed uninterested, was moving off. There was a sigh on the other end. Not even goodbye. "Goddamn it!"

Sunlight off the harbor made the Dock House and other white waterfront buildings glow. The season was coming along. Already a village of sailboats at anchor was starting to form on the other side of the channel next to the salt marshes. What a life, thought Kurt. Pay no dockage fees. Row over in dingys when they needed provisions. All those twirling props on wind generators—free electricity. It was breezy, masts and halyards clanking. Alicia was licking a frozen yogurt cone and looking seaward at a cat sail with bright green and yellow diagonals. Sonny should paint this instead of his little designs, Kurt thought.

"Daddy, maybe we could go out in Sonny's boat again." Alicia was seven, her hair off-gold, like a field of grain.

"Well, he's been busy lately."

"Can we go over to see him tonight after dinner?"

"We'll see, sweetheart." Kurt wasn't anxious to share his daughter, and Sonny had a way of mesmerizing kids with a bagful of magic tricks and amusing stories. Kurt was more interested in learning what was going on with Joan. "Has Mom been talking a lot to Grandpa and Grandma?"

"I guess so."

"Has Daddy's name been flying around the room?"

"Just when we played Monopoly."

"Oh?"

"Mommy said you still had the first nickel you ever earned." Alicia giggled. "Grandma and Grandpa think you're very funny."

Kurt lay in bed. For the past half hour Sonny's dog Blackie, a big Lab, barked twice every twenty seconds. It sounded like *woe, woe.* Sonny exercised Blackie by throwing a tennis ball that often got into Kurt's japanese boxwoods where the dog would always piss on vigorous shrubs that eventually turned yellow. Or he'd leave a pile of turds on the lawn. Joan was always telling him to relax, think of the Big Picture. Whatever that was. *Woe, woe.* Alicia loved animals—Blackie and Tucker, birds and squirrels, even snakes. Kurt was in the backyard, studying her blonde profile as she petted Blackie's huge head. Alicia had a doll's round face, a nose that was small and perfectly shaped with a saddle of summer freckles. Her eyes were large and blue. She pointed to the back door, telling him silently to go into the house, so he did. The first thing he saw was a vase of wildflowers, the orange trumpets of ditch lilies, on the kitchen table. "Daddy, Daddy," Alicia cried. "Mommy and I had fun picking flowers for you, for Father's Day."

"I know, sweetheart," he said, "let me . . . ," but when he turned around, the kitchen and the backyard beyond the open door were empty.

Woe, woe.

Kurt stood in the half dark of the kitchen. The steamy Carolina summer seemed to have set in for good. With the blinds drawn, it was cooler. He and Joan argued often about the most effective way to cool the house without running the AC full blast and driving up the electric bill. Drawn blinds made everything gloomy, she said. Kurt was talking to her on the phone. "I can't talk," she said, "We're on our way to a gallery."

"Then when *will* we talk?" he pushed.

"I'm not sure it would do much good right now."

"Are you telling me you're out of my life?"

"I didn't say that."

"Look, you've been gone long enough now. I miss you, I want you and Alicia back. What's your problem?"

There was static from Joan's cordless. Kurt could see her sitting out under her parent's white gazebo with wedding cake rails and filigree at the eaves. "What do *you* think the problem is?"

Christ, it infuriated him. His mother used to pull the same crap. When he was a teenager, she'd give him the silent treatment for a couple days and when he'd asked what was wrong, she'd say, *"You* know what's wrong." Then he'd play the game and ask what he had done. "*You* know what you did." God, it hurt to think about that drafty house, his mother's paranoia, the mice, the wood stove, and everything else.

"Joan, I was a smoker when you married me, you knew what you were getting into. But I always smoke in the backyard, winter and summer, you know that. And I'm trying to stop."

"I can't talk right now."

"You've got to tell me if there's a future here." Then he said something he regretted even while saying it: "I've got to get on with my life." Joan often laughed at such TV clichés, but worse, without Joan, he knew he wouldn't get on, he'd go under.

Kurt looked down at the trap. The squirrel turned in tight circles, shiny black eyes. It was the one good thing about Joan and Alicia being gone, he thought. At last he could do something about the infestation. The neighborhood was overrun. Holes in the lawn, a nest in the attic, that loud annoying slap as they landed on the shingles. One even came down the chimney while they were out shopping and chewed away some window mullions trying to escape. But Alicia didn't want him to catch and remove all her little "friends." Fat chance—like the Mexicans, they were here to stay. As a kid, he used to hunt squirrels with his father, and his mom cooked them. They saved on their meat bill. When he pointed out a recipe for squirrel stew that he found in the Sunday newspaper, Joan didn't think it was funny. "Why don't you think about your daughter's feelings or someone else's once in a while?"

"I was only joking," he lied.

He drove across the bridge and along a road with pine forest on both sides. He passed a gloomy little family cemetery and turned down a dirt road by a tobacco barn smothered in kudzu. A deer tower stood at the side of a field that was sprouting broad green leaves of tobacco—source of all his woes. After a bumpy mile, he negotiated a steep dip and climbed the other side to a cabin over-hung with boas of spanish moss. The cabin belonged to his friend Stan, a hunter, who was trying to restock squirrels that had once been plentiful.

Lifting the trap from the Taurus, he set it down and watched the gray squirrel frantically bang first into one door, then the oth-er, its nose bloody, unable to figure a way out. "Relax, ol' buddy," Kurt said, "Think of the Big Picture." The squirrel streaked away and was lost among the gray trunks.

The Golf Center was new, out of town, and barely findable, at the end of a white gravel road. Dust from a recent passage hov-ered above the road like ground fog. Four or five true believers were practicing at rubber tees. Six dollars seemed a lot for a buck-et of balls, but you had to spend money to make it. Another guy was nicely clicking out shots that sailed high, seemed to stop against a wall of trees, then bounced on closely shaved humps and swales dotted with white. Kurt envied the guy his swing. And when he began to hit his first balls, he felt how deeply ungrooved he had become. His muscles refused to obey. A sense of inade-quacy oppressed him until he finally hit the sweet spot, and the ball sailed unbelievably high and straight. Then the air offered a happy tang of cut grass, but he flubbed his next shots and felt an even deeper sense of failure. He was sweating. Gnats swirled. Six black cows grazed beyond the road where a car left dust that set-tled slowly, whitely, and reminded him of Joan's filmy nightie, the way she knelt above him, took it off, and laughingly tossed it over her head in the moonlit room.

Sonny waved to Kurt from his roof peak, roiling black clouds behind him moving in off the ocean. Wind had begun to toss the tree tops. Kurt gathered clothes from the collapsible wooden rack in the backyard. With Joan gone, there was no sense using the dryer. Save on the electric bill. He had forgotten how cheaply one can live alone. Not that he wanted to. But nobody else's schedule stood in the way, and the house didn't get messy.

National Weather Service had a crawl on the bottom of the TV screen saying that there were severe thunderstorm and tornado warnings until nine o'clock. Randolph Scott, minus his ten-gallon hat, was pinned down by gunfire next to a watering trough, reloading, trying to figure out his next move when the screen went black. The AC also went silent.

From an upstairs bedroom, he could see Sonny still on the roof. He had a string in his hands. Kurt followed the upward arc to a pair of linked box kites with glittery silver tails that dove and climbed again; one was yellow, the other bright red. The air around them was sooty as the chimney of a hurricane lamp before it went out. Sonny was laughing. The first tracers of rain already made long diagonals on the window.

"That boy smokes too much dope."

That was another thing Kurt didn't do.

Yesterday during the storm, the rain gutters had spilled curtains of water before the windows. Goddamn squirrels again. Kurt leaned the ladder against the gutters and climbed up. He was already sweating. Bushes, grass, cars—everything seemed on the edge of combustion. Twigs and sodden leaves blackened his hands. It annoyed him that he had forgotten a bucket and had to throw handfuls of black glop onto the trim green lawn.

No sooner had he climbed onto the sizzling roof than the ladder slid sideways from his grasp and toppled into azaleas below.

The last person he remembered seeing was Borden, a guy toward the end of the street, heading somewhere on that loud motorcycle of his. While waiting for someone to happen along, he continued to unclog the gutters, coming upon a yellow tennis ball, then a dead blue jay. He wondered if the jay was one he had trapped. Perhaps it had injured itself banging against the wire.

Hands and knees burning, he began to yell for help, discreetly. Neighborhood AC compressors hummed in response. The sun was an angry red. He looked over at Sonny's newly shingled roof. The story of that new roof made Kurt uneasy, but now wasn't the time to think about it. The dormers seemed like unforgiving eyes.

A little kid with earphones and baggy red shorts came up the street. Kurt yelled. The kid stopped and stared at him openmouthed, with impersonal curiosity, as if at a TV sitcom, then laughed and marched away.

Jesus. The shingles were hotter than hell's hinges. Sweat stung his eyes. He might get someone's attention on the next block, so he climbed to the crest. Through a break in the trees, he could see the inlet and ocean beyond. Boats were cool black cutouts, dancing on diamonds of pure sunlight. Alicia kept begging him to get one, even a dinghy, but boats had an endless appetite for money.

Somebody whistled. Thank God. Sonny was coming across the street. "Don't say a thing," said Sonny. "Don't even ask. Dante says that if you see a need and wait to be asked, it would be best if you didn't help at all."

Deeply grateful, Kurt was annoyed—why did he always have to quote somebody?

Angela's face was rosy with reflected candlelight as she plucked a tune on her guitar and hummed. Sonny put down new wine glasses. He had bought a case of Chambertin and wanted Kurt to be the first to have a taste.

Sonny held out one of the glasses. "Do you know what they call this?"

Kurt didn't.

Sonny poured wine into all three glasses. "It's called an 'impitoyable.' That means *pitiless*. The shape of the glass focuses the bouquet and your nose renders a verdict that is 'impitoyable.'"

Angela strummed and hummed.

"Interesting," said Kurt. Amazing the kinds of knowledge Sonny had filed away. But it was all useless, thought Kurt, like his monologues about unmoved movers, names like Pascal and Lao Tsu, the whole nine yards. Gibberish, like Grandfather's German. Sonny's living room was something though—wall-to-wall books, almost no furniture.

Angela stopped playing and took a glass from Sonny. They hoisted together and said cheers. Angela started strumming again. It was hypnotic. The wine was sensational.

"So, how's Joan and Alicia?"

"Well, Joan's mother has these headaches that put her out of commission," Kurt lied. "She's having tests run, and Joan figured she could do some cooking, help out, you know? As soon as her mother gets back to speed, they'll be back. This wine is really delicious."

Sonny's eyes showed candle flames.

Unable to sleep, Kurt realized that the tune was "Amazing Grace."

That new roof of Sonny's, the one he'd flown the kite from— it reminded him of the party where he'd first used Sonny as a figure of fun. With a drink in one hand and a cigarette in the other, he described how Sonny got himself a new roof. As God was his witness, Kurt had tried to set him straight. Don't replaster your living room ceiling, he'd told Sonny, until you get the roof reshingled, the leaks taken care of. Kurt gave Sonny names and phone numbers of several neighbors with newly shingled roofs. See if they were satisfied, Kurt advised. Get estimates. He also mentioned Borden, the guy with the loud motorcycle. Borden worked in the building trades, was an insider, might put Sonny onto someone good, and cheap.

But no. Sonny had the plasterers one day, roofers the next. Very early one morning Kurt heard pounding and scraping. First thing he saw was an orange Gatorade keg tied to Sonny's chimney. Brown, shirtless, and varnished with sweat, these Mexicans were all over the roof, a whole tribe, agile as monkeys. With a big torso and wrap-around sunglasses, the crew boss had a bandido mustache—a mustache, Kurt thought, that neither concealed nor revealed. Leaning against a rusted-out pickup, the guy laughed and yelled in Spanish to *muchachos* on the roof. They were scraping off shingles and tarpaper using hoes with straightened blades. Already they had a good part of the front side down to bare wood, the pink azaleas drooped over with tatters of tarpaper.

Kurt, with his first cup of Joan's good coffee, stood next to the crew boss and watched the show. Sonny came out in swim trunks with a blue and white cooler.

"Aren't you going to stick around, keep an eye on the job?"

Sonny shook his head. "Too much noise. I'm going fishing, drop anchor, and read. You want to come?"

"Sonny," Kurt whispered, "these guys—"

"What about 'em?"

"They don't look professional. Are they bonded? I mean, they're using *your* ladders, aren't they? No ladders of their own—doesn't that tell you something?"

"Man, I'm getting a great deal." Then he said something in Spanish to the boss who laughed and said, "Sí, sí, gracias, más tarde, amigo."

There was no arguing with Sonny. And he'd left his house wide open!

Later that afternoon, at his computer, Kurt noticed that a loud hush hung over the neighborhood. The roofers were gone. The yellowish exposed wood of Sonny's roof gleamed in the sun. They had probably made a trip to the landfill with stripped shingles and tarpaper. Probably lunch, then the ole Mexican siesta no doubt.

About three o'clock, Kurt came to the upstairs window. Half the sky was black, the sun about to disappear behind a phalanx of inky thunderheads sliding toward the neighborhood out of the west. Then it was dark, and even more silent until a breeze kicked up the white undersides of leaves. The Mexicans arrived only minutes before lightning opened the sky. They scurried up ladders shouldering rolls of tarpaper and carrying sheets of plastic. One of them fell off the corner of the porch roof into the bushes. The others laughed. The boss staggered around the front lawn, pointing and yelling. The rain was torrential. It lashed Kurt's windows so hard he could barely see the tarp snap off the roof and fly over the next house.

"They're victims of bad luck too," said Sonny later that night. Kurt stood in the front room, looking at most of the new plaster ceiling in damp piles on the floor. Sonny shrugged, then laughed, "C'est la vie."

Kurt's punch line for the roofing story was, "Yeah, that's life all right, the stoned life according to Sonny." Everyone laughed, said what a character this Sonny must be. Joan, however, didn't laugh, said nothing on the drive home. There was more too, but he wasn't ready to think about it yet.

Kurt stood at the kitchen sink. Tap water instant coffee steamed on the counter, a come-down from Joan's ground French-roasted beans. Kurt now ate over the sink, as he did before he got married.

No mess. No clean-up. In both hands, he held a sandwich and noticed, on a limb near the window, a squirrel with a pecan in both paws. Kurt's jaws moved slowly. The squirrel's jaws moved slowly. They ate watching each other. Kurt stopped chewing. The squirrel stopped chewing. "The little shit is mocking me." Kurt put down the sandwich, his face getting hot.

He was sweeping the driveway, a small pile of trimmings from the weed-whacker, turf from the edger. His bermuda grass came to a perfect right angle at the drive and ran along the sidewalk, straight as the part in his hair. Crickets were loud. He tapped his empty shirt pocket—a reflex that wouldn't quit. Angela was coming across the street with Blackie who would naturally do some watering. Kurt was beginning to see Sonny and Angela as part of his woes.

"Your lawn is so lush," said Angela.

Sonny thanked her and considered the large green eyes peering at him from behind oversized lenses.

"You haven't heard from Joan?"

"Well, every time I call her, she can't talk in front of Alicia, or if Alicia isn't there, she can't talk in front of her mother."

"They'll be back. She probably just needs space. Sonny used to be a counselor, you know. Why not come over tonight, talk?"

"I really appreciate it, but have another engagement," he lied, making himself even angrier. Now he'd have to leave the house for a few hours, spend money for pizza.

It was near sundown. Squirrels were becoming scarce. Without the slap of shingles and Blackie barking half the night, he was sleeping late, sensing, as Wolfie said, a terrible waste of time. It had been three days now since he sent out a résumé or had caught a squirrel. In all, he had relocated sixteen with their country cousins.

Instead of being pleased, however, he was annoyed. Time was losing its shape. The yard seemed horribly empty. Even the red of cardinals and blue of jays were gone. It was as if he had become a cosmic persona non grata. He was unsure what to do. With dread he approached the window. Like an answered prayer, across the lawn, the silver door of the trap was closed. "Yes! Praise the Lord!" He had come to enjoy the repeated ride out into farm country, the release, the orderly ritual.

At Stan's shack, he knelt to release the spring holding the door, but it was stuck. The squirrel turned in tight fast circles. Kurt held the side of the cage to apply pressure to the door, his fingers poking through the wire. Suddenly he felt a hot stab in his ring finger. The squirrel was attached, and wouldn't let go. He screamed and freed himself. His finger was bleeding, the pain shooting. The finger wrapped in his handkerchief, he flung the trap and the squirrel into the trunk of the car.

Past the helipad, he rolled into outpatient parking. Leaning against a gurney, a policeman eyed Kurt, then said, "Way you gone wid that thang?"

"It bit me, and might have rabies. They have to test it."

After a bulky gray woman took his vitals, from last tetanus shot to family insanity, he sat next to three Mexicans. They wore identical white T-shirts, probably from the same stolen three-pack, thought Kurt. They seemed familiar. One had a purple swollen cheek, his arm in a bandanna sling. Maybe he saw them at church.

"Mira eso cabrón," said one.

"Si, con suya favorita!"

Opposite Kurt were two guys talking about cars. The guy with the John Deere hat said, "My cousin, he got him a Trans Am . . . hit this ol' coon . . . flatter 'en bird shit on a Buick!" The other snorted. He wore a black T-shirt that said "Budweiser 10,000 Gallon Club." Now they looked from the squirrel to Sonny.

Sonny held up his hand. "Bit me," he said.

The Budweiser guy said, "Well, that's what you git fo' tryin' to diddle that pore little thang!"

The deadpan Mexicans made them hoot even louder until a nurse called, and they followed her through the swinging doors. Kurt's face broiled. He hoped the Mexicans hadn't understood. Then he recognized them, the roofers who ruined Sonny's ceiling.

The boss said, "Es la suya? Eees dat you leetle fren?"

Kurt said, "I remember you guys. That rainy day, the ceiling on the floor. Right, it's me. So what really happened? Too many beers for lunch?"

The Mexican's dark eyes got angry, indignant. He made Sonny understand that it was *mala suerte,* bad luck, and that his men were not *borracho.* He had two crews, doing two jobs at once. They worked hard. They wanted to do for themselves, not take charity. And insurance paid for the *señor's* ceiling.

"Whoa, I was only joking."

"Yes, beeg joke," said the crew boss. "Sí, chiste."

"Qué chistoso!" snarled the other.

Kurt felt at first that he was living in an anecdote on the build, and these Mexicans would color the telling. But they resisted a version of themselves Kurt had settled on, even painfully altered it. His finger throbbed badly. It was no joke. He felt feverish. Mexicans gone, he was alone with the squirrel, and the looks of other patients.

Dr. Janko was small, had a warm impish smile, and was developing a bald spot that suggested a monk's tonsure. He said that rabies wasn't carried by rodents, not in this part of the country. And in any case this lively squirrel didn't exhibit any symptoms, so Kurt could take it with him. Meanwhile, he was going to beta-dyne the wound, take a few stitches, then give Kurt two injections: tetanus and antibiotic. "It says here you live on Azalea Street." Dr. Janko smiled. "Do you, ah, know Sonny Hastings?"

"Sure, he's a friend of mine," said Kurt. "How do *you* know him?"

"The Bistro. He's a great waiter, very friendly, knows something about everything. He's also seeing a colleague of mine. How's he doing?"

"Why? Has he got some kind of condition?"

Dr. Janko hesitated. "You, ah, said you were his friend, so I just sort of assumed . . ." He patted the examination table. "Please climb up and lie on your back."

His bandaged finger, white, seemed to float in the dark. He sat behind the wheel of the Taurus, not sure what to do first. He felt hot as that day on the roof, frightened too. In three years he had learned little about his neighbors. Joan was right. Sonny was not well. Angela said he had been a counselor. Kurt fumbled the ignition key, seeing himself as others must—a white shirt, loafers with tassels, a guy who straightens pictures in every room he enters. A joker, like the Mexican said. There was a racket on the helipad, figures running, then the chopper rose from its nest of amber lights and swung northeast with nav lights flashing. He watched until the lights disappeared and quiet came back. Frightened, the squirrel made the wire of the cage ping as it moved in quick circles. Cigarettes were the least of it, he knew that now. He decided to cross the river and free the squirrel. Then toss the trap. Talk to Joan. Sonny too.

But first turn the key. As Wolfie advised, one thing at a time.

Bereavement Flight

Judy and I were kicking back, a few drinks with friends. Everything was funny. Jim was mocking a preacher on TV, some guy with teased-up hair quoting Leviticus, pounding his podium, and raging about homosexuality. Jim limped his wrist and wondered about the preacher himself.

Julie couldn't stop giggling. Her glass went *thunk* on the carpet. The preacher's wife wore something like a fright wig and enough mascara to make you think of a raccoon. Kenny said some Florida doctor shot his wife and told the judge he mistook her for a raccoon.

Everyone roared. Barbara said a guy in Connecticut killed his girlfriend, fed her to a wood chipper. The tabloid headline read: "He Loved Her To Pieces."

The phone rang. It was Ned's wife, Anne. Ned was one of my college housemates. He lived up north, in Maine. My heart began to bang away like it wanted out. I got tunnel vision. Ned was supposed to be out of the hospital by now. I'd planned a visit, already had my airline ticket. Hearing her voice, not his, I somehow knew.

Across the living room, Judy's expression asked, *What?* I waved her off like it was nothing. Without even thinking, I told Anne I'd be there. She could count on me. I'd call her back. Sweet Jesus.

I poured myself a drink and hit the bedroom to think. Maybe it shouldn't have been a factor, but cost came to mind. I'm not rich. Two kids in college. I was pretty sure the airline wouldn't rewrite the ticket, one of those supersaver deals. Full fare would be impossible. I knew about bereavement rates from when my mother died, but that meant immediate family only. Still, it was worth a shot.

After an endless Muzak hold, I explained our closeness, Ned's heart surgery, etc., but before I had even finished my spiel, the agent goes, "I'm sorry, that's our policy." A company robot—no tear ducts, formaldehyde for blood.

I thought about driving. Sixteen hours, at least. No way. There were still two other airlines. I dialed again and got this recording saying that my business was important to them, first available operator, etc.

Laughter exploded in the living room. I looked around our bedroom, at family photos, and listened to a classic oldie on the hold recording—"Brandy," by the Looking-Glass, popular when my son was born. Poor Ned. Jesus. Finally this snippy voice comes on and says the same: bereavement means immediate family. Click. Back to Square One. What to do? Lying occurred to me. This guy I work with, Lee, lies about everything and never gets caught. How would they verify kinship? Would an airline rep actually phone the funeral home? *Yeah, this is Suspicion Airlines . . . Are you holding services for a Mr. Ned McDead?*

I decided to try again where I still had that no-refund ticket. I thought about getting pushy the way characters do in certain movies: *I demand to speak to your supervisor.* This time I was connected immediately. The person surprised me by saying, "Are you OK?"

I said, "Not exactly," or something like that. The agent said I sounded out of breath. There was this familiar musing quality about the voice. I couldn't decide whether it belonged to a man or a woman. Everything slowed. You could hear other operators and the tock tock of computers. I gave my name and told the story. The voice sighed, "I'm really sorry."

I said I thought that the immediate-family policy for a bereavement price was unfair. "What about people with no families, just very close friends?"

"I'm with *you*," the voice said. "My family wrote *me* off. Friends are my only family now."

I sipped my drink.

"Excuse, please hold."

I looked at the photos of my son and daughter. What would it take for me to write them off? My son was into piercing, green hair, and hip-hop threads but—

"Sorry. Your friend—he wasn't alone I hope?"

"His wife was there," I said.

There was a kind of listening silence again. Weird and unsettling. Wasn't this what shrinks did? For a second I thought the voice was going to ask me if they had a good marriage, if Ned ever cheated on his wife. Instead, it said, "You stayed friends, that's good."

"Just about every year," I said. "He and his family spend a week on the Carolina coast. That's not far from here, so we get together." But the truth was Judy sometimes thought Ned and me and my other college buddies weren't quite right. After a few drinks, we often got on the phone, sometimes late at night, called each other "Sweetheart," lisped, and pretended to be gay. I found myself saying, "Hey, you ever had a close friend who—"

"Died?"

"Yeah." I drained my drink and listened. There was a hollow sound, like the backwash of surf. The voice finally sighed, "Yeah, more than once."

I decided it was a guy. "Then you know why I've got to get to this funeral."

He started calling me by my name. "OK, Jeff, please hold. Don't hang up, OK? I'll be a few minutes."

The party raged in the next room. Linda was laughing about her minister, a guy who cried in the pulpit almost every Sunday, over almost anything. She did an imitation. For a moment, I hated her. Then Kenny told a joke about Michael Jackson becoming a priest. More laughter. Julie cackling and stamping her feet.

"OK. Jeff, you still there?"

I said I was.

"Good, I've got you set for—" Then the voice got muffled and I heard, or thought I heard it say, *I'll worry about that later.* "Sorry, I've got you set to leave two days earlier. Same flight. No extra charge. Pick up your new ticket at the check-in counter."

I was beside myself. "How did you do that?"

"You delete one number, substitute another."

I said, "I hope you don't get—"

"Not to worry."

"God, I don't know what to say."

"Just remember," he said. "Just . . ."

I don't know whether or not he was going to elaborate but before I could say anything, he switched to a business tone, like a supervisor might be listening in, gave me a confirmation number, and thanked me for flying whatever-it-was airlines.

I just sat there, watching the ice cubes in my glass melt and shift. This guy—he had a familiar voice and tone that somehow got to me. *Just remember.* But I wasn't remembering him or Anne or even Ned. What came to me while I was sitting on the bed—God knows why—was high school, the hallway traffic. One of your buddies would really slug you hard in the shoulder. The rule was you couldn't hit back; you had to pass it on, slug somebody else.

One day this swishy kid, Joey Kitchen, came down the hall and . . . God, that was years ago, and not something I wanted to remember.

Laughter grabbed at me again from the living room. I sat there thinking I could never go back.

Animal Planet

One minute Betty's face is hovering above me, her mouth blowing bubbles that say, *You're not listening.* The next minute I'm alone with Fluff, a bichon frise no bigger than a cat, a white old thing with lethal breath. Then I'm surfing my brother's big screen and treating myself with his Wild Turkey. Time does another hiccup and I'm staring into an empty glass, cubes welded together like a wacky shrinking family. The Christmas lights wink on and off, on and off.

Uncle Bill?

Jesus. The voice gives me a jolt. Stay cool, I tell myself. If I hadn't dropped acid years ago, I might panic. The good lesson of acid is you learn to stay cool no matter what horrors morph into view. I hit the mute button. The ringing silence weighs a ton. Finally I say, What?

Why didn't you go to church with the rest of the family?

I say, How about this? The nearer the church, the further from God.

Nothing, then the refrigerator kicks on. Hell, I've wasted a good line on a dog, on an empty room with a flickering TV screen. High and squeaky, the voice has got to be Fluff's. She hates me because I know she's spoiled. I don't cut her any slack. She bit me once.

Taking no chances, I put her into the courtyard. The clinking of her collar buckle and license tag gets on my nerves. Now the only thing to disturb my surfing is Betty's echo: *You're not listening.*

The Spanish I hear in every store or gas station out here makes me think I've crossed the border. Maybe I have, but this new country is a place where fewer things matter. There's a certain lost freshness. Ever since I hung up my spurs last year, the world seems less substantial. No underlings to ask for my signature or well-informed opinion. There are huge areas I no longer give a rat's ass about, if I ever did: NFL playoffs, our senator's love child, or what the Nasdaq is doing. My father spent most of his days outdoors. My mother had a massive coronary watching a soap opera, an empty bottle of vodka on the floor beside her chair. *Qué importa?* My mother has vanished almost completely, but my father doesn't realize he's dead. This morning he was pointing to the top of a cottonwood, squinting, trying to help me spot my first bobcat.

Every year Betty and I come out here to visit my brother Mike and his wife, Mary, at Christmas. A tradition or a habit of some thirty years. Now that the children are grown and gone, the old board games have been replaced by bridge. I'm not much for games, so they have this widow friend of theirs come over, a churchy person named Dotty, an active pro-lifer with hard opinions on everything from arms control to the architecture at Angkor Wat. Betty has always liked cards, so it works out well for all parties. Mass and a little bridge for them, a long hike for me.

Whenever I can, I put the binoculars, a bottle of water, and a few snacks into the knapsack, and head for the desert, which pretty much begins at the end of my brother's street. There's a deep arroyo at the back of the house that follows the curve of Camino Ocotillo for a hundred yards then veers away toward a high mesa. Last year I met these bikers when I was walking the sandy bottom.

They invited me to stop by their shack for a beer. They got a kick out of calling me "Pops." They probably liked me because I wear a gray ponytail and took a few hits on their bong. *Hey, let's take Pops for a chopper ride to our connection in South Central.* This year the biker shack is vacant, the windows smashed. As I circled the place, two coyotes on long legs watched me from a distant rise of greasewood scrub. Coyotes are moving back into the city. My brother sees them on the golf course. You spot them around dumpsters in back alleys. Earlier in the week, after mailing gifts to our kids, I spotted three of them slinking out of a culvert near the post office where a dry wash goes under the road. They're opportunists, like Australian dingos, know how to stay alive. Yesterday I saw a docu about a dingo that carried off this couple's baby while they were having a picnic.

I switch to NBC and *Dateline.* There is a segment about three football players in Iowa who broke into an animal shelter and used baseball bats to kill twenty-two cats. The cats were all strays and worth under five hundred dollars, so the ballplayers were convicted of a misdemeanor and fined, lightly. In this community of farmers, a man with a fat face seethes into the camera: "For cripes sake, they was just cats, that's all they was, worthless stray cats. These boys got a bright ath-a-letic future to think about and now some cat-lovin'—Hell, she went and ruint everything."

I splash myself another Wild Turkey and look into the courtyard out back. A tall eucalyptus and a big saguaro with two nubby arms like a cross. The surface of the swimming pool is covered with long thin leaves. Years ago, the pool would be lit like an emerald. After we decorated the tree, my brother always turned on the pool-heater and our kids would be out there yelling and doing cannonballs at each other. This year nobody is flying out for the holidays—a first, and a genuine area of avoidance. My son Jeff claims he has to work. Ditto for Jennifer, a nurse. My nephew and niece have other excuses. Only old Fluff is out there stumbling around the half dark pool, barking at ghosts.

Two decks of cards wait on the kitchen table. What if I removed a card from each deck?

Fluff is just about blind but must have seen my shadow. She's thumping the patio door, which makes a racket. I let her in and she wants to know if I'll open the dishwasher so she can lick the dinner plates clean. No? She senses there is no court of higher appeal. Where has everyone gotten to? I tell her they're still at midnight Mass.

But it's only seven o'clock.

Well, it's a pretend midnight Mass. What the hell do I know? She gets on her hind legs with her front paws together, but arthritis won't allow her to pray anymore, and she flops down. My niece, Amy, taught her the praying trick when they were both pups. Fluff is really Amy's dog. But Amy and her husband couldn't manage a dog when they were in law school and med school, so my brother—who is not really wild about animals—and sister-in-law end up with Old Doggy Breath.

Same thing happened to me and Betty, but with Jeff and Jenny's cat, Minou. They went off to college, and Betty and I inherit this orange cat. She had been with us for seventeen years until I put her down last Christmas before coming out here. Renal failure. Common in cats, especially old ones. Betty was long in denial. I came downstairs one morning and Minou was lying on her side in front of the fridge. She could barely lift her head. We had been trying to rehydrate her, but it wasn't working. Skin bagged from her bones. Her food untouched. No wet spots in the gray litter of her box. This was it. I got the picnic basket we always used to transport her to the vet, talking all the while to keep her calm, telling her how Hemingway loved cats, and explaining our country's appalling lack of a coherent foreign policy. I'd love to have a recording of all the conversations I had with that cat. So as not to wake Betty, I whispered and slipped out the back door with the picnic basket.

So there's Fluff waiting for her prayers to be answered. "Here you go," I say, flipping the Tasty Treat, which bounces off her head. I keep forgetting she's nearly blind. She just stands there staring before she starts to sniff for its whereabouts. I finally have to put it into her mouth. Then back to surfing endless channels on the big screen. My brother's done well for himself. His house is huge, cavernous. Fluff makes her way to my knee, her collar clinking. She can't make the jump anymore and waits for me to lift her.

Uncle Bill, I thought you were a practicing Catholic.

Hey, pay attention. You're repeating yourself like a true geezer. Listen up. Sisters of Mercy, Franciscans, Jesuits—from kindergarten through college. Christ, that's enough practice to last me a lifetime. I don't need the practice anymore! I know the routine, got it down cold! OK?

I stop at the Animal Channel. It's the story of this vet who adopts a dog from a client no longer able to afford the animal's cancer treatments. The vet reads up on cutting-edge protocols and sets about trying to save it. We see how his family loves this Irish wolfhound. The thing looks to be about the size of a Shetland pony. The vet closes down his practice, buys an RV, and moves his family to a midwestern city where a university school of veterinary medicine is pioneering methods to treat various kinds of canine cancer. The children are uprooted, put into new schools. Even treating the dog himself, the vet ends up spending ninety-five thousand dollars in what is finally a losing battle. I'm thinking: I retired never having gotten anywhere near ninety-five thousand. Anyway, the vet's wife can't look at the interviewer any longer. She turns away, mascara running in inky streams down her cheeks.

Fluff is scratching at the door. Jesus H. Christ, I say. Didn't you just come in?

But, Uncle Bill, I want to show you something.

Show me what? That you can take a wiz outside instead of on the kitchen floor? I leash her up. Out the back door, through the pool area, and out through the wooden door in the adobe wall. It's desert, not much smell except a tang of wood smoke from people burning their fireplaces in the valley. Cold. No wind.

We climb down into the arroyo and head toward the old biker shack. The stillness is deep. Just the sound of footfalls on the hard packed sand and stones. A few days ago I had seen a Harris hawk circle, then go into a stoop. Up she flapped from behind a soap-tree yucca, with a rodent clutched in her talons. Lights of Tucson to the east. There's a big moon, cactus flats dappled with black shadows of small clouds drifting east. The yip of a coyote not too far to my left, an echo from another further off, then a longer howl. Fluff stops. *Uncle Bill, where has everyone gone?*

Where have all the flowers gone? That's a '60s tune. Do you realize you're repeating yourself, I say, or are you just trying to break my chops? I could see my brother, Mary, and Betty at this outdoor mass at Santa Cruz. I went to those things once upon a time with the whole family, but the effect isn't what you might expect. Instead of silence and magi stars, you get all kinds of jet and chopper noise, sirens and, worse, a lame-ass sermon that even Spanish can't disguise. Then there is the traditional and obligatory tour of certain neighborhoods known for their ooo-and-ahhh Christmas lights.

This is better. I'm sitting on the mesa, under big stars. The moon makes everything very bright. *Uncle Bill, is Amy coming home?* I let go of her leash. She sniffs and squirts here and there. *What about Jeff and Jenny?* I'm watching a shiny black beetle of some size climb up a bank of sand. Something makes me want to tip him over with a twig. So I do and watch him on his back, six pairs of legs churning in the air. *I haven't seen Amy in a long time and that makes me very sad.*

Jeff used to come home for Thanksgiving. He and I always swam together and along the way there were milestones. In his senior year of high school, he beat me in a freestyle race. Hard to accept. Let's try it again, I said, and really poured it on the second time, but the result was the same. In college, when he came home, he showed me a new lifesaving tow, not the old cross-chest carry or chin-pull. I was high on his chest, face far out of the water, while he was mostly submerged. His kick was pure power. We walked home from the pool, the route we always took. When we got to the steep grassy embankment by the insurance company, he gave me a shove, and I had to run with the momentum all the way to the bottom. He stood at the top, laughing and slapping his thighs. "Dad," he said, "that's payback for all the times you pulled that dumb trick on me when I was little." We laughed and shoved each other the rest of the way home. Later we had a beer and watched a college football game. I remember him sitting on the sofa playing with Minou, dangling a string for her to paw at. When Jeff dozed off on the sofa, the cat climbed into his lap. I crept out of the room for the camera and have a photo of them slumped over in the same way, both catnapping.

When Fluff and I get back to the house, the churchgoers and Dotty are into a game of bridge. They shuffle, fan their cards, study the table, make their bids. Fluff and I are invisible. Dotty is outraged that our president got his weasel greased in the Oval Office. She is looking forward to the execution of the Oklahoma Bomber. She thinks that a murdered abortion doctor in upstate New York got what was coming to him. The country needs prayer in public schools. I know my brother is doing a slow burn. He doesn't like talk and card-play at the same time. I make myself a drink and, in the middle of Dotty's rant, I turn on the TV to a spaghetti western. Henry Fonda, dressed in black, with evil blue eyes, is about to gun down a sweet red-headed child in "Once upon a Time in the West." A demented harmonica is starting to wail.

Dotty says, "And everywhere TV has taken root, crime and addiction have risen. The entertainment industry is a moral sewer. Trash like that"—she points at Fonda who slowly works a cud of tobacco and spits—"really offends me."

She looks right through me. I've taken her on in the past. I'm not one to mute my views, but I surprise myself by saying nothing. After a few minutes I get up to refill my drink and generally observe that Christmas always brings out the best in people. My voice sounds dubbed, as if it doesn't belong to me. Dotty's lips move but what she says doesn't reach me. Dotty used to be sweet. I think of that beetle I tipped over struggling to right itself, legs working uselessly.

Where was I? My sister-in-law is saying, "—something to show you." Great. I want something to look forward to, but maybe that's a mistake. I wanted Dotty gone, but she's only gone to the bathroom. Fluff had had something to show me too. What was it? Stars? An overturned beetle? Everyone shuffles to the game room. Their new computer sits on a desk next to a ping-pong table long unused. My brother opens some e-mail attachments. Photos have just come in from Amy and her husband: shots of their new house in Maine, the snowy yard and trees. Then a shot of their very own first Christmas tree. Betty takes my arm. "Remember our first tree?"

Jesus. I say I do, but I'm sure our memories are not the same. My parents were upset we wouldn't be spending Christmas with them. Sunday was designated for my ritual phone call home. Week after week, my mother would give me the silent treatment. Her silence lasted for months. Dad handled my calls, steering me away from any mention of the problem.

The final attachment is a photo of Amy and her husband holding a Yorkie pup. Very cute. Light reflects in its warm dark eyes. He could be a detail in a painting by Renoir or Goya.

Uncle Bill . . .

Fluff wants to know what we're looking at. I tell her it's an electronic picture of Amy and her husband in their new house with a new puppy, a cute little Yorkie, their only child, for they have decided against the human variety. Why lie? What is it the kids say? *Get a grip. Get over it.* Fluff turns and limps from the room, her license clinking against the collar buckle.

The house is silent. I'm alone with my empty glass and melting cubes. I'm giving the remote a hell of a workout. The story about the football players in Iowa, the cat killers, is on again. When the vet put Minou under, there was a look of abandonment in her eyes. Her breath shallow. The second needle of potassium chloride stopped her heart. I hadn't expected to sob, but I did. After Dr. Gray wrapped her body in a towel and put her back in the basket, he told me to sit in his office for a while before driving. Lots of pet owners, their worlds blurred by tears, apparently have accidents after such an experience. He put his hand on my shoulder and told me I had done the right thing. Lots of owners make their animals suffer because they can't face the inevitable. So I shouldn't feel bad about myself, he said. As if we're not pros at forgiving ourselves for just about anything. I finally got in my car and drove. Somehow I discovered myself later sitting in the airport parking lot, Minou's body next to me on the passenger seat.

I find a big puddle and several smaller ones on the kitchen floor. Fluff stands nearby, aimed in the general direction of the living room and the lit Christmas tree. *Uncle Bill, when are Jenny and Jeff getting in?*

I try to ignore it.

Uncle Bill—

I tell her to shut the fuck up. I open the door. She stands there looking at me for a minute, then moves into the pool area. She follows me to the wooden door in the high adobe wall. It's colder now and this is where things get tricky. Are we going for a walk again? I forget what I told her. I hear a coyote. Fluff doesn't. Her hearing is probably shot, like everything else. The door creaks open on its hinges, late-night quiet making everything louder. The house behind me is dark but for the flickering light of the TV. I look back at the house, but I'm not sure what happens after that. Do I shut the door? All I hear is a quick yelp, snarls, and the rattle of gravel stones beyond the wall. When I turn about, I see a gaunt, long-legged dog that after a fuddled moment becomes a coyote. I glimpse something like a limp white bundle in its mouth before it slips down into the arroyo out of sight. I run a few feet, stumble, then stop. Oh Christ. What can I do? It's too late. I let something horrible happen. Maybe it's just an acid flashback? But a sudden cold wind that quakes the palo verde branches is real, not part of some dreamscape. The heavy wooden door grates horribly on its hinges, back and forth, back and forth.

Shutting down the big screen, I move to the Christmas tree. A few needles come off in my fingers with a strong scent of resin. I tug a branch to make ornaments clunk and tinkle, then pull the plug. When my eyes adjust to the dark, I slowly climb the stairs, knees cracking.

In the bathroom, I look at myself in the mirror. I try to smile, my canines more like yellow fangs than ever. My fingers smell of sap. I wash them with soap and rinse with cold water, splashing my face too. The house seems very cold. After brushing my teeth, I hurry under the covers with Betty. My movement stirs her from sleep. "God, you've been drinking too much," she moans.

"I know."

She sighs. "What possessed you to make that crack about getting the Yorkie baptized and raising it a pro-life Catholic?"

Jesus. I don't recall saying anything like that. I know it's possible though, and say I'm sorry. I want to tell her what happened to Fluff, but that's impossible. I'm suddenly too tired even to think, never mind talk. Betty snuggles against me and says we should go out into the desert tomorrow with our field glasses. She's read up on hummingbirds of the Southwest and knows a few places where we might be able to see some. She whispers, "'Living jewels,' the book says." She mumbles something else before her breath becomes rhythmic and deep. I lie awake for a long time trying not to think, but thinking nonetheless about what I have done and not done. I whisper, *Living jewels, Living jewels,* as if it were a prayer, until the dark becomes complete.

Yellow Tom

Sometimes a theme will haunt us for weeks. A few days ago I was reading a bit of bedtime trash involving a cat—"The jet black creature with red eyes crept along—" and a scream ripped the dark beyond the bedroom window. A week ago perhaps, walking past an overgrown lot where a house once stood, I heard something like a groan, someone in trouble. I stopped. The sound grew in pitch, became a scream, and two smoke-gray cats exploded from the brush. One chased the other to the edge of the lot. They tangled, for a moment became indistinguishable, then fell into a deadlock of intense staring from a distance of no more than a few feet. For several minutes, I watched them. When I returned half an hour later from the neighborhood Fast Fare, they were still locked in their bluff, so alike in their smoky looks I could have sworn only one cat contemplated its other self before a mirror.

Three days ago, a friend who lives down the street telephoned and said he had something to show me. His voice was excited. When I got there, he was in the backyard looking into a big wooden box with a wire mesh top and a trapdoor. A yellow tom with a huge head and a tail thick as a raccoon's gazed up placidly at us. The last time I had seen him was months ago lying in the bushes next to my back door with a chewed ear and a bleeding gash on his head. There were tufts of yellow fur mingled with tufts of black fur all over the lawn but no sight of the black adversary. All night the two had kept me awake with their hiss-and-howl routine. I felt like kicking him, but he was too beaten even to worry about my approach. Finally he found his feet and with slow dignity made his way toward the woods beyond our back fence.

"Where did you get that trap?" I asked.

"Humane Society," he said. Then with a boyish grin: "Stick your hand in there."

"Sure. What are you going to do with him?"

"Let the Humane Society put him out of his misery."

I said he didn't appear to be in any misery.

"No, but I am. He tore up my Siamese. The vet's bill was seventy-five bucks."

I shrugged.

"He tore up your cat too. What, you goin' soft?"

"It's my son's cat," I said.

"That may be true, but it's your money."

Bill reminds me of my father. He's kind to people, unsentimental about animals. Practical. Like the farmers we lived near in France. Once, a youngster in our village sent a dog sailing off the fender of his Peugeot, took off without stopping, and left me with a peasant woman to watch the dog twitch and bleed its last among poppies in a roadside ditch. I muttered something about the poor dog. The woman snorted, put her hands on wide hips, and fixed me with one ox-eye: "Mieux la bête que moi, Monsieur." There was irritation in her voice and it put me in mind of the irritation my mother and I often produced in my father when it came to animals. Growing up, I had several dogs which my father did his best to ignore. He had been a farm kid and simply couldn't fathom pets, giving table food to a dog, keeping it in the house where it could shed hair on the furniture, vomit on the floor, or worse. Returning from a Sunday visit to my grandparents' farm, we would sometimes enter the living room and sniff something amiss. Our white-haired mongrel, Miss Jones, was cowering in a corner, tentatively wagging her tail, testing an approach. "Wonderful," my father would thunder. "Just wonderful. Well, you and your mother wanted this mutt; you clean it up." As he'd leave the room, Mom and I, grinning conspirators, tried to stifle our laughter. When we would hear him again on the stairs with a crack—"God Almighty, they eat dogs in Korea!"—we would be unable to contain ourselves, and he would say, "Keep it up, someday you'll come home and it won't be here." Instantly sober, Mom would shout at the ceiling, "Don't-you-ever!"

Looking at that tough yellow cat, I wondered what Mom might have said to Bill. She had always been a sucker for dogs but later in life when her legs gave out and a dog became too much of a chore, she transferred her affection to cats. I no longer care much for either, but something about that cat almost had me by the heart. Almost. Because Bill was right. The tom had cost us and it *was* a nuisance. I left him loading the box trap onto the tailgate of his station wagon.

Cats. I've gone from active dislike to indifference. My school friends and I used to take pot shots at them with our B-B guns, howl with delight when we would get a four-foot leap or a painful scream. But that wasn't dislike; it was simple adolescent cruelty. Dislike came when, as a college student, I cat-sat for the first and last time and Annabel Lee, as she was called, landed on my chest in the middle of the night with her claws bared. Because the bedroom door hung crookedly in its frame and couldn't be shut tightly, the cat once again landed on my chest. Fifteen minutes later. I chased her around the apartment, cornered her, got deeply raked on the arms, but locked her in the bathroom. The capture took almost an hour because I was groggy with sleep and a belly-ful of teenage beer. Annabel's owner was my English teacher, a tall, daffodilic young man. At that insecure time of my life, I developed the idea that a liking for cats, fuzzy pastel sweaters, or colors like baby blue could only mean one thing. That did it. For years I saw nothing interesting about cats and made the most absurd infer-ences about people who owned them.

More recently, when we moved out of an apartment—where there was a rule against pets—into our own house, my son asked for a cat. Of course I resisted. But with wife and son in alliance, I relented. Actually I was glad he didn't want a dog because we trav-el a good deal and a dog cannot fend for itself as easily as a cat. So we got a kitten, which quickly became a cat, a small calico of in-side/outside disposition. Outside is where the problems came. Cats are territorial, spray a perimeter, and defend it, often fool-ishly. Our calico is courageous, but most other cats in the neigh-borhood are considerably larger. After our first forty-dollar trip to the vet, I bought a Wrist-Rocket, closed the circle, and became a kid again, remembering my father's stories about hunting rabbits with a slingshot during the Great Depression. I didn't want to kill any of these intruder cats, so to sting them I used cop-per B-Bs rather than big lead pellets. With a leap and a yowl, they would be gone over the back fence. My calico, thoroughly un-grateful, would emerge casually from her recently embattled po-sition under the car and begin licking her paws as if nothing had happened; the intruders would only return the next day—whether out of defiance or stupidity I could never tell.

After leaving Bill and the trapped yellow tom, I drove out to the coast and over the new bridge onto a barrier island where we rent a cottage every summer. The ride is only an hour and usually pleasant but it was cold, and the sky over the flour-white stretches of dune and beach was purple-black. Wind buffeted my small car, and most gulls were glued to rooftops or stood in groups behind dunes. Unusual for Easter week in these parts when families invade the island to line up a place for the summer.

The rental agency was in an old third-row house. I stood in an overheated smell of kerosene and listened to the sign outside creak wildly on its hinges. Since I hoped my father would fly down to spend a beach week with us, I told the young woman behind the typewriter I'd like to see a few three-bedroom places. There was a smell of cigar smoke mixed in with the stifling kerosene and I wondered where the owner was. He was officious, irritable, and often fought with his wife in front of renters. Just as well he wasn't around.

I drove slowly. A view of the ocean was blocked by rows of stilted cottages that bore names like "Enchanted" and "Happy Days"—names made ironic by the weather and wind that was ripping a carp flag somebody had left flying at "Jonah's Place," a place of potent decay and gloom not even Lysol and the bright weather of months to come would dispel. The place that fit our situation perfectly ("The Cat's Meow") had been broken into. Intruders had come in through a door giving onto the deck. Splinters of glass glinted from the carpet in dim light. Beer cans were scattered about and all the beds had been romped in. A condom floated in the toilet.

Back at the rental office, the cigar-smoking owner blinked at me as I relayed the information. The young woman was gone and he sat behind the typewriter with a big tawny tomcat in his lap. I was surprised on a double count. I never suspected, given his disposition, that he had a cat. In summers past, I had heard him threaten renters with the consequences of keeping pets in cottages. In the office for my mail or a phone message, I'd suddenly find myself facing him across the counter, the warned party gone, and knew I'd be the ear into which, for some reason, he had chosen to confide his dark views about people: you don't judge a person by what they say or how they dress, no, you look at the cottage and the kind of shithouse they've left behind; you judge by the bounced checks, by the way they come here to cheat on their wives, or men to sleep with other men. Oh, no, I didn't have any idea what pigs and slobs most people were.

Knowing his feelings about people, I was surprised to see him lovingly stroke the cat. The tom lay on its back, eyes glazed and staring at a great marlin leaping on the knotty pine wall, as the owner absently scratched its furry gonads. "You know," he asked, "what they ought to do to the kids who broke into that cottage?"

He didn't wait. As he outlined medieval measures, his scratching of the cat became more vigorous. Boldly, I distracted him, brought him back to the business of a down payment and reservation. The cat gave me a malevolent look when it hit the floor. I watched the owner cross the room to a file cabinet. There was a path in the wine-colored carpet, the design nearly gone. His step no longer had spring. I hadn't seen him since last year and finally realized what I had been too distracted to notice—that his hair had gone completely white. He had lost weight and loosened flesh hung in wattles from his jaw. "Oh, I don't know, I don't know." He shook his head. When I was signing the agreement form with all its stipulations, he lighted one of the cigars that his wife, during the summer, forced him to smoke outside. I wondered where she was. "What's your hurry?" he said, pulling a bottle of Rebel Yell from the bottom desk drawer. "Here, have one for better weather." The cat stared at me from the corner, narrowed its eyes. I told him I had to be on my way.

Pure cold air washed over my face and was a great relief to the lungs. As I passed the window, he was tipping the bottle, the cat already on the desk.

Before leaving the island, I pulled into an empty parking lot next to Captain Kirkland's Fishing Pier to watch big waves chop and heave along the desolate quarter-mile span of wood, then thunder on the shifting shoreline. There was movement, color, perspective given by the pier—a lot to watch, lose myself in. Like being at a drive-in to see an improbable film. A few gulls rose and hung like momentary kites; their wings flashed white against rolling purple clouds. My attention was drawn to something moving on the asphalt, a cat, a big white cat with a few black markings. It stopped, looked at the car, and slipped through a hole in the skirted part under the pier house before I realized that the cat, with its facemask and limp, was stunningly like my mother's. I stared at the dark hole. There was a brief white gleam behind the opening. I wanted another look.

At first I saw nothing, shadows and beams, sand and the shine of an imperishable beer can. The smell of brine and weed rot was boosted by something else. A movement finally adjusted my eyes. Perhaps a dozen cats looked at me looking at them. They were, according to the proverb, all gray in the dim light, but gradually began to define themselves: gingers and blacks, short and long hairs, an orange tabby, a calico like mine. Even a costly Siamese had come to this fallen state. Then they were alike again in their gauntness and scruff. They weren't Cheshires, but they seemed to vanish behind yellow smoldering eyes and drove me from the hole.

I was glad to get back into the warm car and wondered if I really saw the white cat that reminded me of Mom. It wasn't to be seen under the pier. And it was too fat to belong with them unless it had been recently abandoned. In summer, with plenty of fish about, the pier was Fat City, but how did they get through the winter when everything was closed? Wondering if there wasn't something wrong with me for wondering, I pulled from the parking lot, fed a cassette to the player, and let eighteenth-century Salzburg surround me with a better theme.

The rest of the day was mercifully cat-less, but that night I dreamed about the white cat with black markings. I desperately wanted to see it and found myself crawling through that hole in the lath skirting under the pier house. Once through the opening, I was in the basement of my father's house. I could hear hushed voices and lonely organ music from Mom's afternoon TV programs. Dad was at work. The chair thumped and her footsteps sounded above me. "Come on, sweetheart," she said. The cat would be waiting on an entry platform my father had made for it. I heard the window open and close. "That's a good girl. Mama loves you. Come on, get you something to eat. That's right." I followed overhead footsteps to the kitchen. The cat's dish scraped as it left the floor. There was a long alarming silence, a choking sound and a groan. Then the thunder of my mother's body meeting the wood overhead. I bolted up the cellar stairs and yanked at a door that was locked. I called to her, banged on the door, listened. Faintly but urgently she was whispering my father's name and mine. I tried to shake the door but someone was holding my hands. My wife was saying, "It's OK, it's OK." And slowly I recognized our darkened room.

My workday was unusually full and kept me from thinking about cats, even kept me from habitual moments of dreaming and staring at intricate branchings of a grandfather live oak framed by my office window. I was walking home when Bill called me from his yard. "I couldn't do it," he said.

"Do what?" I asked.

"You know," he said, "gas the tom."

I laughed. "You getting soft?"

"Right after you left, my son came home. He persuaded me to take the cat somewhere and drop him."

I asked where and he told me they put the trap in their canoe and paddled across the river. He said it was the easiest, most humane thing to do. The cat would have to go twenty miles up or downstream to a bridge.

"Wanna drink?"

"Got to get home," I said. I liked Bill, but our friendship had fallen into a rut.

Midway up our hill, the Jermans' red setter ran into the street to meet me with a stick. It was a ritual of throw-and-retrieve until I reached our yard when he would trot back down the hill. Friendly dog. Social, like my old Miss Jones who made friends easily, wagged her tail, and played with other dogs. Cats aren't that way. They patrol the driveways, porches, and hedges of their precincts, wary, suspicious, always ready. And when together, as they were under the shelter of the pier, they existed under a fragile truce, preferring no doubt to be alone.

On the kitchen table was a note: "Went Shopping. Children With Me. Your Dad Called. Sounded Strange. Back Soon. Love, XX." I made myself a drink and thought about the call I would make in a moment. With my mother gone only a few months, nothing was the same anymore. New worries took the place of the usual, trivial ones. Until the funeral, I had never seen my father cry. It wasn't tears that worried me, it was the change. Physically sound, he was now emotionally brittle. With few friends and me five states to the south, he was radically alone. Before my mother's death, his countless acts of love made the word foreign and unnecessary, but now "love" was often in his speech, and I was uncomfortable hearing it. A few days after the funeral when we pulled from the driveway and headed south, he waved to us from the porch, holding the cat in his arms.

The cat's name was "Bobbie." It was the only word I could first make out. There was static on the line and his voice cut in and out as if a record were playing and the needle couldn't track the warps. Finally I realized he was crying. Distance distilled sound and made it pierce unbearably. I talked, tried to calm him, discover what had happened, but I was far from calm myself and "Humane Society" was the phrase that pulled me out of my fearful imaginings, forced me to listen. It seems he had taken Bobbie there two or three days ago. The director assured him they would find a home. He took all of her things, bell-ball, scratching post, everything. A month's worth of dry and wet food.

"Dad, why, why did you do this to yourself?"

He began to sob again. "God, you don't—I miss her so much."

Once again, I asked the question.

"I couldn't keep her, I just couldn't keep her."

I said I didn't understand. Then with a sob that confused things, he said she was strange. Or it was strange. Though both were vaguely true, neither was an explanation. But I decided not to press further because my questions were evidently upsetting him. We talked instead of his recent visit with my aunts, of his forthcoming visit with us.

"Maybe he didn't want to impose on anybody," my wife said when she got home.

I asked her what she meant.

"You know, to take care of the cat when he comes to visit us."

It was a possibility. It's also a possibility that the cat reminded him too much of my mother, that the cat behaved strangely now. There were many possibilities and many alternative courses of action he could have taken. I suspected he acted out of some kind of panic. My wife agreed. She suggested her brother—who lives in the same town on a farm not far from my father—retrieve the cat so Dad's act need not be irrevocable. But first I had to call the

Humane Society. I checked my watch. There might still be somebody there.

Repeated rings produced an irritable voice. "Yeah, yeah, I remember him. Old guy. Left in a hurry so's he wouldn't cry. They all do it. Big white cat with black, yeah, scratched the hell out of me."

I asked if the cat was still there.

There was a pause. "He brought that cat in over a week ago."

A week? Dad had told me two or three days ago. "Well, did you find it a home?"

"I'm afraid not, pal."

"I happen to know my father left a month's worth of food for that cat. Why did you give it only a week?"

There was no reply. Then: "Look, pal, sometimes we can't even place kittens. What can I tell ya? That cat was trained to one person. It scratched me good."

"But you had a month's worth of food," I said, "You could—"

"Look, we got policies to abide by. What can I tell ya?"

Angry, I said, "Nothing, pal. You've told me everything you know. What can I tell ya?" And hung up.

It was getting dark. I stood there looking out the back window toward the fence and tangled upper branches of the woods beyond. In the other room my wife was watching TV news. There were floods in the Midwest, thousands homeless, an economic recession, record unemployment, social service cutbacks, a war raging in the Falklands—all this and I could think of nothing but my mother's cat, the problems it posed. My priorities seemed wrong. But at least I could do something about the cat—or so I thought before I called the Humane Society. Perhaps something still. In any case, I told myself, certain offices must be observed.

The phone call took place hours ago, and I've been thinking of those offices. When I was ten or eleven I got my first B-B gun and before long shot a robin off the telephone wires in front of our house. There were bright droplets of blood on its rusty breast, but it still had a pulse, opened its beak. I picked it up and ran sobbing to the house, put it down on the back steps, and barged inside. My father, still sweaty and dirty from work, stood at the kitchen sink with a glass of ice water and listened to my gasping story. I put my head on the table and cried. When he came back inside, he put his hand on my head and told me to stop. It was all right, the bird was all right. The robin had flown weakly to the top of our chicken coop, rested a while, then made it into the woods. As I wiped away my tears, Mom took over with a lecture about cruelty and killing and how she was against the B-B gun from the start. Bloodstains on the cement steps met me when I went out to play a bit more before dark, but there was no sight of the robin and I felt feather-light with immense relief. Many years later my father recalled the incident and told me he had simply dropped the bird in our trash can.

It's late. I'm having a nightcap, thinking what I'll say to my father when I call him tomorrow. Everyone's gone to bed. I hear a sound that is like a child crying—a soft but insistent cry that strikes deeply and momentarily freezes me. I go to the back door and hit the driveway floodlight and there is my calico, ears flat, back arched, fluffed up and aimed at an unseen enemy on the other side of my car. I open the door and she streaks in, glad for the chance to escape. After a few moments the yellow tom with that huge head and fat raccoon tail moves from behind the car. I laugh in spite of myself and step out onto the back porch, but he doesn't scare. Not even when I descend the stairs. He simply pauses in the middle of the yard, licks his paw once or twice, and gives me a disdainful glance. I think of running for the Wrist-Rocket, but something else in me just wants to watch him measure the fence, flow with incredible grace to the 2 × 4 at its top. He looks at me once again. For some reason the name Monk comes to my lips. I call him that. Perhaps because Thelonious, the great jazz man, has recently died. A real bad cat, as they say. Stay out there, Monk, make difficult love, wild unregenerate sounds.

Junk Trade

We were briefly back in Connecticut—the loose ends of my father's estate. I had stopped on a dirt road that leads to the dump so that David could take photos of muddy hogs and flights of pigeons with his new Minolta, but he was taking forever. It was hot and the stench of the piggery was awful. I whistled, told him to hurry. We had a carload of stuff to get rid of. Hogs sent up the pigeons again; they flickered in the sun like scraps of white paper.

In the car, he said, "Dad, do you think Mom will do it?"

"We've been over this," I said. Rachel, on a whim, had applied for a job in Atlanta, and a week ago received notice she was a finalist.

"I don't want to move."

"Maybe you won't. She could fly home for weekends."

"Weekends!"

I had already explained to him the importance of his mother's work, her need for a sense of self, and saw no point in further talk about something still so iffy. "Let's just bury it for now. We've got other things to do."

"Slow down," he said, leaned out the window, and aimed his Minolta at the DEAD END, each bullet hole burning with light. He clicked off a few frames, and we turned from the tree shadows onto a sand and gravel track that came to a fence. In the open, just beyond the gate, was a man at a desk with cinderblock legs, a breeze riffling pages in the ledger before him. "He's asleep," said David. The guy had hair the color of a Brillo pad, wore overalls and a faded work shirt. Our tires popping gravel jerked up his head. As I cranked down the window to a gust of rancid heat, he squinted at me through smudged lenses taped at the bridge and lifted his hand against the sun. A younger version of the face came to me from years ago when, as a college flunk-out, I had worked for the town on the back of a garbage truck. It was Louie, but he gave no sign of recognition when I used his name. Instead, absurdly, he yelled, "Halt," heaved himself up from the chair, and hobbled toward the car with that limp I had forgotten.

I told him I had newspapers, a Hoover, wire coat hangers, rags, a recliner, a small AC unit.

He looked me over suspiciously and moved to the rear of the car as if to see for himself what was under the rope-tied trunk, but in the side-view mirror, I could see him check my license plate. He came back shaking his head. "Residents only—that plate says Georgia."

I explained that my father had recently died. I was cleaning out his house.

He was still suspicious.

"You could look it up," I said, pointing to his ledgers.

He hobbled around the desk. "What was that name and address?"

I told him. He licked his thumb and began to flip pages. The offal-haunted, green buzz of flies came from an open dumpster a few yards off.

"Jesus, Louie. It is Louie, isn't it?"

He said yes.

"If I wasn't *from* here, how would I know your name?"

Looking up from the ledger, he lurched back to the car.

I asked him if he really thought I'd drive all the way from Georgia to Connecticut just to get rid of junk here in the town dump. Hanging his face in the window, he said he was sorry, explained that space was the problem. Supply and demand. Other towns had run out of landfill space, were jealous, had even tried to sneak in truckloads at night. The town had to be careful.

I nodded. The impression was apocalyptic, garbage wars in the offing. When his speech was over, I changed the subject. Still wanting to establish myself as a former workmate, to prove something to my son perhaps, I ticked off names and asked for news. "What about Watrous?"

"St. Mary's, pushin' up daisies."

Stunned, I quickly moved to Phillips.

"Danbury." This was a euphemism for prison. "Stole some TVs," he said. Then with a smile: "He oughta be gettin out pretty soon."

Finally I came to Steen, the other kid on my truck.

"Doin' real good. See that?" He pointed to a mountain of junk. "He's in charge of the whole metal pile. You'll see him when you drop that AC unit." Louie was getting tired of my questions. "The rest can go in those dumpsters. Make sure you separate it apart into the right ones—paper, cloth . . ."

We drove ahead.

"Dad, how did Grandpa ever accumulate all that stuff?"

"How did you ever accumulate all that junk in your room?"

He laughed. After explaining what a milkman was, I told him how my father would be on his route before dawn, the first to see interesting things people put at the curb. I didn't want to recycle a cliché but found myself using what my aunt, more than once, had said yesterday at our yard sale: "One person's trash is another's treasure."

"Dad, that's dumb."

"Why?"

"I'd never touch anybody's trash."

"Never say never."

"Yuck, no way."

I told him that my father used to say you never know when something will plug a gap, fill a need.

"What about all those baby carriage wheels hanging from the basement ceiling?"

"Sure. Remember the red wagon with high sides he made for you when you were little?"

"I guess."

"Where do you think the parts came from?"

We got out of the car. I told him how, just as he had pestered me for that new Minolta, I had once pestered my father and mother for a boat because we lived close to a lake. Like most kids, I was selfish and didn't realize what they couldn't afford. But one lucky spring noon, I was knocked over by the sight of a green bow sticking out of the roped rear doors of the Divco my father delivered milk in. A ten footer, perfect for two or three kids, it was missing oarlocks, a few floorboards, needed caulking and paint. My father could repair anything. I could still see him smiling: that somebody thought the boat worthless made him all the more happy.

David pinched his nostrils. "Dad, how about later?"

The smell was potent. "That's perfume," I teased.

Into the dumpsters went a bolt of canvas, two boxes of clean rags, stained lampshades, a box of inner tubes. David held a big boxful of comic stationery. "Hey, why are we getting rid of this?"

"Space," I said. "No room in the car."

"Gee, I like this paper."

"Take a few sheets."

"How about this much?" He held up a five-inch stack. "What's so funny?"

One day my father took me and two of my seventh-grade pals to the dump. Such trips were always adventures: BB guns and rats. But the purpose of this jaunt was to throw away two orange crates full of records, old 78s that my mother's friend Sophie had left behind when she took a job in Detroit. Years had passed, and still they remained unclaimed. From Sophie, no Christmas cards, nothing. For my mother, bewilderment turned into hurt. "Don't say anything about this to your mother," I was told with a wink, and we loaded the trunk of the Studebaker. At the dump's landslide edge, we spent a wonderful hour in a contest to see who could fly records the farthest. Out sailing over the cattail swamp went these black discs with titles like "Mammy" and "Tabby The Cat" and "I'll Be Seeing You." Redwings stirred and flitted, plummeting records made an abrupt rip when they knifed water or mud. But I recall as well that my father refilled those big orange crates with other things while "I'll Be Seeing You" and hundreds of other silent melodies sailed briefly over the waters of forever. We left with more than we brought.

"Dad, I really don't want to move to Atlanta. All the time on TV news, you see these drug addicts, murders, everything."

"David!"

For a while he was quiet. Then: "Dad, do you think that pile of refrigerators and stoves would make a good photo for the Boys Club contest?"

"If you get the right angle," I said.

"How about the way the road winds up to it?"

The orange bulldozer that had been clanking and grinding suddenly shut down and a hush hung in the air like a new smell. Seagulls wheeled over hummocks in the smoky distance where, from even further, came the long moan of the Sandy Shoals foghorn.

Back at my father's house, when Johnny, my cousin, pulled into the drive in his Grand Sierra pickup, I went out to meet him. Hid-

den from view were two blond children, his wife-to-be's from a
first marriage. A Vietnam vet with lingering problems, he had, after a series of menial jobs, taken courses and now was working for
a company that made turbines for the navy. To everyone's surprise—and my aunt's relief—he was getting married; in fact, the
wedding was just a few days off, and he had come to pick up bedroom furniture. Rachel knelt before the children and asked them
if they would like to sit on a swing bench that hung from the big
oak out back. Sucking thumbs, they nodded yes.

Together and singly, Johnny and I made trips from house to
truck until both bedrooms were empty. When I was carrying the
dresser mirror, David backed and crouched, clicking off some
kind of trick reflection shots. The truck was full, but I brought
Johnny into the cellar and pressed some of my father's tools on
him. "How about a saw?" I asked.

"OK, I'll take one."

"Come on, he's got ten."

Johnny laughed. "Uncle Pep, he was a good guy." He talked
about how my parents had looked after him when his father died,
tried to help him out when he got back from Vietnam. "You
know, sometimes I'd hang back about stopping to see them because there was no way I could leave without a meal or some
money, and while your mother had me at the table, Uncle Pep
would be loading my car on the sly. A TV, food, paint, tools,
sweaters, gloves—you name it."

Our eyes paused at the twelve-gauge Remington I got when I
turned fifteen; it hadn't been fired in years. I knew better, though,
than to ask him if he wanted it, or the .22 semi-automatic that
hung just above. Johnny's eyes were clear blue and deep, like my
uncle's, and looking at him, at the flared cheekbones, I could see
my father too. I wanted to talk, but there was no time. And his
children had become bored with the swing bench.

Behind the wheel, he leaned forward, waved, and tapped the

horn once as the truck began to move. The load was well balanced and tied. My mother's mattress was almost new, satiny white, and strewn with cornflowers that slowly vanished.

Eduardo, an old friend, lived just a few miles from my parents' house. Whenever we came to Connecticut, we spent a lot of time with him, and now that the phone in my father's house was disconnected, Ed was taking messages for us, and we were using his phone, a new one we joked about because it specialized in dialing wrong numbers, had a cricket-like ring, and might, we suspected, be a secret test item on a new line of disposables like razors, lighters, and flashlights. When I told him of our difficulties getting rid of all the junk, he laughed. "Oh yeah. Anything beyond your two standard barrels, you've got to practically gift wrap, or they'll leave it in the street."

"Hey, when I was a lid-lifter—" I began.

"You'd take it all, right?"

"True."

He gave a mock sigh. "Ah, the deterioration of services!"

I told him I had seen a few of the old lid-lifting crew and that Steen was now in charge of the whole metal pile.

"You should have had more ambition," he scolded. "You always had more on the ball than those other garboonies. Today you could be King of the Dump, ruler of an empire."

"What did you do with the phone book?" I asked.

Ed, ever the self-mocker, said, "Out in the kitchen, on top of the metal pile, I mean the paper pile."

I found the directory and began flipping pages. Rachel was telling Ed about being a finalist for the job in Atlanta. Ed said, "But you've got a perfect situation where you are, don't you?"

"Well, Michael's position is secure, and there's a kind of Podunk happiness." She laughed. "I do some part-time consulting."

I called the Salvation Army about disposing of what remained from the yard sale. The house had to be emptied. Soon. In barely a week, David would start school, and I had a job to get back to. A woman's raspy voice said: "People used to bring in the leftovers of yard sales. Junk really. We can't accept that stuff any more." Her voice was like a recording.

I explained that it wasn't junk. I had a good easy chair, a hassock, sheets, blankets, mattress covers, dishes, lamps . . .

"Well, if our truck comes to your house for pick-up, insurance prevents our driver from climbing or descending more than two steps—Excuse me, will you please hold."

Muzak came from the receiver. I looked at Ed's kitchen. Clean but cluttered, it looked like mine before I got married. On the floor was a red and white DieHard taking a charge. My eye followed another power cord to the baseboard next to the cellar door: it was a small black speaker that emitted barely audible squeaks and had a chrome plate that said Super-Bug-Away. In the living room, Rachel and Ed were talking about politics. Over a drink or two, they could argue for hours. Ed was sunk in his wingback, a two-foot stack of magazines and newspapers next to the chair. Paperback novels, video and audio cassettes stacked on every flat surface. David was fiddling with the stereo, ears muffed, head nodding rhythmically. Ed held up *Cancer Ward,* then dropped it on the floor. He was saying, "See? Now he's a non-person here too. Remember the Harvard Commencement when he said Americans had speedboats and snowmobiles instead of souls? Remember? We didn't like that. And now some guy's written a book about the anti-Semitism in his work." Ed smacked his lips. "Kiss of death. He might as well be back in a Siberian gulag."

The Muzak stopped abruptly. "As we were saying, insurance prevents—"

"Yes," I said, "I heard that."

"The other thing you must realize is that what will be taken is completely at the discretion of our driver."

"You mean, he might not take everything."

"That is correct." Her voice was metallic.

"Great. What if we bring it in ourselves?"

"I can't make any promises."

I walked into the living room and repeated the punch line. Ed quaked with laughter.

David removed the headphones. "What's so funny?"

"Listen," said Ed, "even the dump won't take certain stuff. Last spring, I had accumulated a lot of ashes from the fireplace there, drove out to see your garboonie pals. 'Forget it,' the guy says. Who's the one with the limp and gin-flowers on his nose?"

"Louie," I said.

"Well, Louie said he was sorry. But it happens I had just been to the package store. I figure, why not? I offer him a beer. We shoot the bull for a while. Between sips, he puts the can on the ground. 'I could get fired for this,' he says. Another beer, he starts to soften. 'The hell,' he says, 'dump the ashes over the bank. Anybody comes, make believe you takin' a piss.'"

"Nothing like getting your ashes hauled, huh?"

Rachel begged with a smile, looking furtively at our son.

"Remember when your old Ford gave up the ghost and Whaler Wrecking gave you twenty-five bucks for it?"

Ed said, "I know. Now I'd have to pay *them* twenty-five."

"At least."

Rachel, interested in an article, asked if she could take the magazine.

"Sure," said Ed, "but bring it back."

I looked at the cover. "This is three years old."

"I know, but there might be something I missed."

I asked if he wanted my rifles.

"Why not? If Super-Bug-Away doesn't work, I can just blast away."

The house was becoming horribly empty, but I could still see my parents in their favorite chairs, or moving about as usual. The temptation was to idle and mope, but there were too many things to be done. I was wondering how we would get my mother's rocking chair and my father's power tools and other odds and ends into the car. Geometry was useless. We would have to rent another car, or a small van.

"First things first," said Rachel. "Let's get this stuff to Salvation Army and take our chances." So the three of us loaded the car, David reluctantly putting aside the Minolta. Halfway into town, I passed an Avis and turned back. The woman, chewing gum, asked me why on earth I wanted to go to Georgia, what with the heat, the drought, and the racist rednecks. She loudly snapped her gum for emphasis. After she told me there would be an additional two-hundred-dollar drop-off fee, I wanted to tell her a few nasty truths about Our Town, but the shortness of time pushed me out into the squinty sunlight again.

A thin man at the Salvation Army was smoking, giving everything an appraising look. Because there was no loading zone, I had to park down the street in front of an adult bookstore and carry every bursting box down the sidewalk. Sweating, I brought the last one into the store and set it down with the others. Between trips to the car, I kept thinking about how the thin man had casually slipped a Willowware serving platter from a box of dishes and slid it under the counter. He didn't know I had seen him. I remembered that platter from a Thanksgiving dinner, the set it belonged to. Until excused, my cousins and I weren't allowed to leave the table, and I remembered studying, out of boredom, the plate pattern—the pagoda with its tile roof, the blue birds, the bridge, and the boat, small with perspective, bearing the tiny lovers away. Suddenly that platter could have been solid gold, especially when the thin smoker complacently said he'd take everything but these pillows.

"Why?"

"Not healthy, somebody else's head's been on 'em."

"What about"—I gestured to all the used clothing—"that?"

"That's different," he said. "Besides, it's a state law."

"Fine," I said, "you're the boss."

I waited until he gave me the receipt. Then I went around the counter and retrieved the Willowware platter. I never use the word "sport" with strangers and was surprised to hear myself say, "Sorry, sport, I changed my mind."

Our car wasn't quite big enough for the extra things. Things—the kicker. Much of me wanted to leave them. My problem was that I couldn't just drive away empty-handed, and, my father's son, I rebelled against the absurd fee for a one-way rental car to Georgia. Ed laughed. "Hey, why sweat a few bucks? The house here's going to sell. Rachel's going to be making big money." At his kitchen table, I sat with the yellow pages, dialing one car outfit after another—even "Rent a Wreck"—waiting out the Muzak holds and blankly staring at the Turner reproduction that Ed, oddly, had hung over his stove, all the yellows and reds making me think of a grease fire, of the thin smoker, self-combustion. On one endless hold, I hung up.

Ed handed me a beer. "You know," he said, "I'll bet you could get an el cheapo airfare for Rachel and David, put on the max allowed for luggage plus a few extra well-tied boxes at—what?—a few bucks each, and that way you'd be able to fill the car, front seat and all, and not need to rent another, as they say down there in the land of cotton, 'vee-hick-cul.'"

Rachel and I looked at each other. He was right.

It was a two-hour ride to the airport in Hartford. The ponds, hills, and stonewalls stayed with us most of the way. Very different from the flat red fields and walls of Georgia pines we now called home. Rachel talked about Ed and laughed. "He hangs on to all those old magazines. What a pack rat!"

David said, "Why does he keep all his stuff in the kitchen?"

Rachel said, "He's that kind of bachelor. Your father was like that too."

"And you saved me." This was our joke.

"Disorder is the punishment for disorder."

"Super-Bug-Away!" We were laughing. Then the airport sobered us with all of its spaghetti ramps, signs, and various kinds of parking; it had grown unbelievably. From the air, it must have looked like an insult, a new bubble in the strangled ganglia that was Hartford. I parked in front of the terminal. To my surprise, the person at check-in said nothing about our rope-tied boxes. Off they went on the conveyor belt and disappeared through a mouth of dangling black snaggles.

"Three days at the most," I said, giving her a hug and kiss.

"I feel bad about leaving you," she said.

"Don't."

"Dad?"

When I turned, he snapped a picture.

Normally I enjoy driving alone, but now I didn't. Once a pick-up passed me with furniture piled in the back. Another time, I came out of distant thoughts, and a few feet away was a kid riding shotgun in a Trans Am. I had apparently been gesturing and talking to myself, but before I completely registered his mocking face, the driver tromped it, and the car made the leap into hyper space.

Back at the house, I filled a Seagrams box with loose photos and family albums and a few things my mother could never let go of: one was a whale-oil lamp with a hand-painted chimney that her father had brought back from Japan. I especially wanted to keep her coffee mug with the blue tulip—made by a potter friend of hers—and planned to warm my hands with it in winter as I came slowly awake.

When I finally went into the kitchen, I found Ed had been there. A note taped to the refrigerator said: "A call for Rachel. The Atlanta deal. A Ms. Sallie Fearing said it's good news. Call by Friday about an interview. Tel: 912 . . ."

I thought about the joke where the doctor tells the patient: "I've got good news and bad news . . ."

The afternoon quickly slipping away, I met briefly with the realtor, serviced the car, and bought some cassettes for tomorrow's long trek. A kind of panic had me speeding. Calm down, I told myself, and walked around the house, under the great lovely maples and pines. In the soft saffron light, as if out of *The Road Warrior,* a goggled man in a homemade gyrocopter flew low over the house, making an awful racket. For some reason I'll never know, he circled, then hovered. Though my father might have admired the mechanical ingenuity, he would have been shaking his fist at the noise. I stood on the lawn and shaded my eyes. Finally, after slowly rotating the craft, he banked and disappeared over the trees.

It was time to organize what, tomorrow morning, would be loaded into the car—the rocking chair first, then the Sessions clock, then the other things cushioned around it. The cellar still held enough junk for one more trip, but naturally the dump was closed on Wednesday. Next to the garbage barrels at the curb were neatly stacked paint cans, a few wooden crates filled with rope, springs, and milk cartons full of used roofing nails. Six rickety TV tables. This was as much as I dared put at the street. The rest I would dispose of after dark.

Not much more remained to be done. The light was almost gone. I pulled the plug on the refrigerator, propped a broom against the door to keep it open, and grabbed the last can of beer. Sweating, I looked at the empty rooms and knew I'd need a few more beers. It was quiet, the kind of woodsy quiet my parents liked: birds, a rabbit or squirrel rustling leaves beyond the stone wall, the occasional drone of a light plane. Every room was empty. I'd sleep on the carpet in the front room tonight. The realtor was a family friend, and I could expect a good price for the house, but that meant little. In Georgia I often thought about my parents, but here I could feel their presence. I knew every mood of air, every nuance of light and sound. The creak of a floor plank produced an image of my mother coming down the hall with the evening paper, the scrape of a sauce pan, my father making her coffee.

The quicksand had reached my neck when I noticed a blue Nissan pickup pass the house several times, each time slowing. At first I thought it might be one of those yard sale people come back for some item he might get, by now, for a steal. On the third pass, one guy leaped out, grabbed the six TV tables next to the garbage cans, and flung them into the back. Then the other peeled rubber as if having just robbed the First National Bank. Surely they had been sent to save me. I thought of Ed and began to laugh. Then the foghorn sounded in the distance, mist hovered over the swamp across the street, and I knew I had to get out before my mother did a nightwalk from her bedroom or my father floated toward the street to retrieve his goods.

I killed the motor and lights. The upper stories of the new Town Hall were fuzzy in the settling mist—only a few office windows, here and there, framed with light. Crickets were loud. The dumpster I had parked next to had the town's name stenciled in white. What I was doing couldn't have been illegal, but the closely watched dump and the stringent pick-up regulations had forced me into this nighttime stealth that suddenly had a dangerous feel to it. I was behind enemy lines, and nervous. To make matters worse, the dumpster was empty, and every time something hit the bottom, a great hollow boom reverberated in all directions from the parking lot. I was sure the building facade would blaze with light any minute now. Just as I was lifting four wooden jelly kegs from the car trunk, a pair of headlights swung around the corner from the direction of police headquarters.

Sweating, I froze and watched the beams, given solidity by the building fog, slide and lance through trees, then disappear into a glare that made me squint. The cruiser came on and stopped just a few feet away. A voice from within asked me what I thought I was doing. Didn't I know this dumpster was for the exclusive use of Town Hall personnel? Did I know the penalty for breaking local ordinance #2605? As directed, I walked toward the open window, and another light hit me in the eyes. He wanted a driver's license. Slowly he spelled my name, then made me pronounce it. "Funny," he said, "I used to know a jackoff by that name," and got out. "Hey, it's me, Joey!"

We laughed and shoved each other. He told me he had seen the Georgia plates at the house and had been planning to stop, shoot the breeze. The radio crackled. We swapped some history, tried to bring each other up to date. He had two children and was on the verge of promotion to detective. Then back to the present: "What, you trying to get the dumpster into your trunk?"

I explained, and he looked closely at the jelly kegs.

"Don't throw those out," he said. "They're oak. A little cutting—they make nice magazine racks." He was putting them into the trunk of the cruiser when a call came from the dispatcher.

"Gotta go," he said.

I asked what it was.

"Domestic disturbance," he said. "Come on, see what the world's really like."

I told him I had a few errands to run and invited him to join me later at the Bird's Eye.

The Bird's Eye was empty, bright, and as bad in its own way as the house. Beyond the brilliant green of the pool table, booths and stacks of beer cases lost themselves in the half dark. Cars, fog-dimmed, passed slowly in the plate glass. It was like being in a Hopper, but Harold had a sense of humor and liked to fill the air with talk and laughter. On the TV was a special about Hollywood's Golden Years.

I took my second beer to the pay phone and called Rachel. She seemed excited about the job interview, but not overly so. I asked how her flight was, and she asked me about last-minute business with the house. We agreed there was no sense talking long-distance about ifs. Yes, I'd pull off the road if I felt sleepy. We made our usual good-byes.

Harold said, "Yeah, Joey's a good man, smart cop, too smart to come in here." He laughed, picking up my glass. "Another?"

I nodded.

"Ed tells me you're hard to beat on flick trivia."

The beer was starting to work. "Hey, one person's trivia is another's treasure."

"I'll test you for a beer," he said.

I told him he was on, and with his best Mexican accent, he said, "Badges, we dunt need to show no stinkin' badges."

"Every moron knows his Bogey flicks," I said. "You must be trying to hustle me."

"Name the actor then."

I knew it, but the beer wouldn't give me access.

"Bedoya, Alfonso Bedoya," he said, theatrically snatched one of my damp bills, and drew himself another beer.

When it was my turn I said, "Hut, hut, hut."

"Too easy. I'll just give you the stars—Pat O'Brien and Ronnie Reagan."

"Wrong."

"Wrong? We're talking about *Knute Rockne, All American,* aren't we?"

"No, we're talking about *Lawrence of Arabia*—O'Toole to the camel."

He waved me off. "Wise guy. That white lightning they got down there's doing funny things to your mind." He set another beer on the bar and asked me when I was going back. I told him I was leaving in the morning. On the TV, an old clip showed Doris Day singing "Que será será," and we started laughing again. Harold said, "Remember the flick where she's a stewardess and Hugh O'Brien, the pilot, is hurt bad and she has to land this big four-engine job?"

"*Crowded Skies?*"

"I'm not sure."

"Only so much junk you can keep in your head, right?"

Harold didn't laugh, and that made me somehow self-conscious. Suddenly I thought I might be in too good of a mood. I had no food in my stomach, and the beer had given me a boost. I thought about calling Ed to thank him and say good-bye, but over the years we had avoided that kind of direct leave-taking, and I'd probably see him within a year anyway. I looked at my watch. Joey, I knew, wouldn't show up. For a while I thought he would. Tired,

I'd shut myself off after this one, creep home through the fog, and sleep on the living room floor. For a pillow, I'd wrap my running shoes in a towel. At dawn I'd be on the road, plug Freddy Hubbard's "First Light" into the cassette player and let that hard-driving tempo take me down the Connecticut Turnpike and past New York. After Jersey, I might get the sense of possibility that a long drive always provided. But there was still tonight, this bar, Harold, some laughs. Don't think about anything else, I told myself.

And for a long time, I didn't.

About the Author

Photo by Ric Carter

Peter Makuck is a Distinguished Professor of Arts and Sciences at East Carolina University where he has edited *Tar River Poetry* since 1978. He is the author of an earlier collection of short stories, *Breaking and Entering,* and five volumes of poetry. His essays and reviews, stories and poems have appeared in the *Hudson Review, Sewanee Review, Poetry,* and the *Laurel Review.* He lives with his wife, Phyllis, on Bogue Banks, one of North Carolina's barrier islands.